Merie Vision Publishing
Merievisionpublishing@gmail.com

Copyright © 2025 by Jeremy Jae Jae Davis
Uptown Classic Productions

ISBN: 978-1-961213-21-0

Library of Congress control number on record

This is a work of fiction. Names, characters, places, and incidents either are the product of the author's imagination or are used fictitiously. Any resemblance to actual persons, living or dead, events, or locales is entirely coincidental.

All rights reserved. No part of this book may be reproduced in any form either by electronic or mechanical means, including information storage and retrieval systems, without written permission from the publisher, except by a reviewer who may quote brief passages in a review.

Formatting, Editing, and Design by
Merie Vision Publishing, LLC

Front Cover by Che'Von

First Print Edition: June 2025

Printed in the United States of America

# Keisha :
## The Fall Of A Dynasty

Jeremy Jae Jae Davis

# ONE

The two-bedroom luxury condominium sat just 23 miles north of Buckingham Palace. It was there where she stood in the middle of her living room floor, speechless, as Montano, the Jefe of the Mexican Mafia, exited her residence along with five of his armed henchmen. He left her with 2.5 million in cash and his personal phone number.

*What the hell just happened?* she thought, looking out of her $12^{th}$-story window as the men entered their luxury Range Rover motorcade. It had been a stressful two years not knowing if she was going to die or not. It felt surreal that she was still alive. She still couldn't believe it, but Montano gave her his word and had assured her that she was good.

It was finally over, and she could breathe and live the life she so desperately worked so hard for. With the need to calm her nerves, she reached inside her purse and retrieved a single Newport and one of her favorite cherry marijuana gummies. She looked in awe at the heavy bales of money that had been decorating her bedroom walls for the past two years...now, finally hers.

▼

**Three Years Later...**

Keshia walked out of the Saks and Fifth boutique, escorted by her security detail, after her two-hour lavish shopping spree. She often shopped before making business deals. It always seemed to ease her mind. At her convenience, the store manager would shut the entire store down the moment she arrived, allowing her the comfort to shop while having the full staff cater to her every want and need.

After a little over an hour, her bill came up to around a hundred thousand dollars in just shoes, belts, and purses. She ran out of time, but scheduled to return the following Monday. Today, she was on her way to meet up with Imani Davis, the notorious Queen Pin from Virginia, who happened to run the East Side Projects in London. She also happened to have several high-ranking narcotic DEA agents and a handful of prosecuting attorneys in her pocket.

Her father, Aveon Davis, was legendary. He was known for being one of the top shootas of his generation. Unfortunately, he was killed shortly after his release from federal prison, but due to his unwavering loyalty to his cartel, his daughters, Imani and Sage, were financially secured for life. They were left with millions in cash along with his cartel connections.

Keshia's initial plan was to link up with Imani so they could expand their drug operation and take back all of England. Thus, pushing every other drug ring out. She knew that would be a cakewalk, but there was just one opponent standing in their way. The infamous Racheal Mendez, aka Kandy.

After learning that London was the new melting pot and a lucrative goldmine, Kandy and her rebel cartel, led by her insane son Jah'mille, planned on invading London. They wanted to take over the city's surrounding west side territories and flood them with their massive drug supply of pink cocaine, heroin, and fentanyl. She knew her and Imani's drug cartels combined would be a force to be reckoned with. She also realized that a lot of lives were at stake, but for the money, power, and respect, she was willing to pull the trigger on Kandy's mission. She just needed Imani and her La' Familia cartel to agree.

She reflected back on how their friendship went sour and laughed. She could recall a time when Kandy was willing to do anything just to be like her. Now, she was sitting on her high horse, looking down on everyone. What Kandy didn't know was that it going to be a bloody war in the kingdom if she thought for one second that she was taking over any of their British territories the way she once did back in the States. Kandy's greed had always been her Achilles heel.

She was currently running several drug operations in Texas, Atlanta, New York, Philly, and North Carolina, but this time, she was operating on foreign soil. There was no knowledge or resources coming from the UK. That gave Keshia and Imani the upper hand and a stronger advantage. She knew it wasn't going to be an easy task, but for some reason, she also knew the possibilities were inevitable.

Her phone rang.

"Hello?"

"Hey hoe!" Keshia said.

"Girl, you crazy," Imani replied, laughing.

"How you been, sis?" Keshia asked.

"I'm doing well. Me and the guys are out here in Chesapeake."

"Can we link up?" Keshia asked.

"Of course."

"Great. I'm en route to you. By the way, I ran into Montano last week."

"For real?!" Imani replied, excited, remembering how he just up and disappeared.

Montano had taken a two-year hiatus after his father, Ceaser, the Jefe of the Mexican Mafia, was indicted and arrested by Federal Marshals for war crimes against humanity, sex trafficking, kidnapping, and murder, all while running a drug enterprise. Those two years had shortened their drug supply and clientele, which gave other drug rings the opportunity to infiltrate the westside territories. They flooded the streets with synthetic opioids, stepped heroin, and baked-up cocaine, but all of that was finally about to be over.

"I'm all the way psyched! The last time I checked, the westside territories were starving," Imani said.

"And from talking with Montano, it's about to be Thanksgiving in June," Keshia replied before ending their call.

They happened to link up five years ago when Jah'me, aka The Black Ghost, held an all-out exclusive cartel meeting at his castle in the secluded hills of Newhaven, Connecticut. Ever since, they had been inseparable. It was rare to find another Queen Pin on her level who could also relate to her outside of just drugs and money. They bonded like sisters. They talked almost every day. On Fridays, Imani held karaoke and game nights. Tuesdays were taco and book reading night. They would both sit, read, and discuss their novel while eating cheese and drinking some of the finest wines. Things you wouldn't expect two female drug lords to be doing, but that was just their way of staying mentally focused in a drug underworld run by powerful men. In all, it was a dirty and stressful job, but they wouldn't have wanted it any other way.

▼

Jah'me was leaving the African District Attorney's office with his son Jah'mille by his side.

"Listen, Pops, I did pull the gun out, but I promise I didn't shoot anyone."

"But you still beat the man's brains out of his skull with the gun, son," Jah'me replied, shaking his head. "You just refuse to do the right thing. Jah'mille, you're going to have to grow the hell up! The District Attorney's office is tired of your antics. The violent acts you've committed as an adult would have gotten the average Cape Town citizen a life-plus sentence. It's coming to the point where my reputation won't be able to get you out of your foolishness!"

"That's impossible, Dad! Look at you! One of the FBI's most wanted, and you just walked straight out of a crowded African District Courthouse full of pigs. That's some dope shit!"

"But you're not me, son, and watch your mouth!" Jah'me yelled. "I don't care how grown you think you are. Don't ever curse around me again."

"Yes, sir," Jah'mille replied.

"That's exactly what I mean. You're putting me in danger coming here, but once again, you're not thinking about Pops, huh?" He stopped walking mid-sentence and looked at Jah'mille. "So, you really think I'm some sort of untouchable superhuman, huh? You see where El Chapo and Puff Daddy are? Money is nothing to the Feds, son. They print it. When they want you, there's no paying your way out. I've been telling you the same thing since you were a teenage boy. It's time you left the nest. Your comfort and lack of respect for the law are insane to me.

The definition of a man is a person who takes accountability and responsibility for his thoughts and actions. It's time to put aside your childish ways, son. I hope and pray there won't be a next time. If so, I will not be extending my hand. I suggest you go and hire some legal counsel for any future mishaps. I'm withdrawing my staff and legal team from anything that has to do with you criminally from this point on." He shook his head in disappointment.

"I've been saving you so much that you're starting to feel untouchable. And nobody walking God's green earth is. You have become a danger to yourself and a liability to our family empire. I expect better from you from this point on." Jah'me ended their conversation while taking a few business calls for the remainder of their ride.

Ten minutes later, his champagne-colored, bulletproof 2026 Maybach 650CLS arrived at his helipad, where his eight-passenger luxury helicopter awaited. Several of his armed security stood looking like the men in black. Instead of laser guns, they held FN 5.7 hollow-point handguns and wore top-of-the-line body armor.

Jah'me hugged and kissed Jah'mille on his forehead before exiting the vehicle, leaving him sitting and pondering his future decisions. He suddenly came to the realization that his father had just washed his hands of him. Jah'mille hated disappointing his father. He knew for a fact that his father was more upset with him than he appeared to be. He was always good at masking his temperament—a quality he knew he should have embraced. He felt awful knowing his father had flown three thousand miles and ended a multimillion-dollar business deal to personally get him released from police custody. He knew he had to change his ways before it was too late. They met eyes one last time before Jah'me's helicopter disappeared into the bright blue African sky.

▼

**Great Bridge, Chesapeake, VA**

Keshia pulled into Imani's luxury eight-bedroom estate, where she was welcomed at the door by armed security and Imani's son, Christopher. Over the past few years, Imani and Baby Chris, aka BC, had gone from being business partners to becoming the first Black power couple in Caesars La' Familia Cartel.

"Hey, Auntie!" Christopher said, running up to hug her. He was taller than the average ten-year-old, and he looked exactly like Imani, with long, curly locks hanging down his back like his father's.

"I miss you," he said.

"I miss you more," she replied.

"Where are your parents?"

"My mom and dad are both in the backyard. Dad's cooking on the grill and my mom's swimming in the pool."

"Follow me," he said, holding her hand while walking her down the long corridor.

Upon arriving out back, Keshia noticed that Baby Chris was standing at the grill, and Imani looked to be lying on a green float, sunbathing while talking on her phone in their gigantic Olympic-size pool.

Baby Chris approached Keshia with a hug, then pointed in Imani's direction.

"I'm going to need one of those plates, brother," she said, excitedly looking at the food layout.

"I got you, sis!" Baby Chris replied.

"I see you over there getting that vitamin D, girl!" Keshia said.

She sat at the edge of the pool, kicked off her stiletto heels, and dipped her feet into the cool water. Then, she reached into her purse and pulled out her Dior sunglasses. She was definitely feeling the summertime vibe.

"Shit! Not the vitamin D I really want!" Imani responded while sticking her tongue out at Baby Chris, laughing.

"Stop being nasty," he replied, walking toward Keshia and handing her a plate full of barbecued beef, chicken, and ribs.

She quickly said her grace before stating that her food didn't stand a chance.

"So, what's the numbers on the supply situation?" Keshia asked.

"I was told around five metric tons were coming through around the first of January. We're just going to have to find a shipper to get it from JFK to England," Imani said.

"I just may have a few options. What is the most you're willing to negotiate for the shipping cost?" Keshia asked.

"My top offer is a hundred million. No more, no less. For that much, I can fill a fleet of banana boats for ten percent of that!"

"I feel you, sis! But what percentage of our shipment will actually get past the Coast Guard or even customs? We have to pay to play. That's our reason for teaming up. We can't come in expecting losses. England has become a melting pot, and every cartel wants in."

"So, what are your plans with Kandy?" Imani asked.

"Girl!! That's a topic for the round table. Right now, I'm just going to relax and enjoy the rest of my evening and eat."

▼

Jah'me's company, Davis Builders Industries and Incorporated, built and designed modern marvels. They specialized in historical landmarks, theme parks, and arenas. The Las Vegas Raiders' new AT&T Wireless Arena was just one of his recent projects. Also, the newly built Los Angeles Clippers basketball arena. His current project was the Notre Dame Cathedral in Paris, where his team of architects, craftsmen, and stonemasons helped to renovate the iconic interior after the devastating fire in 2019. Jah'me's genius mind and professionalism earned him the trust of French President

Emmanuel Macron and the respect of business associates worldwide.

His schedule was hectic, making his time valuable. As much as he loved his son, he loved himself even more. He sat and thought about the lifestyle he diligently worked so hard to provide for his family, and this was the thanks he received. His ex-wife, Kandy, was literally out of control. Ever since their divorce, she had become a cold-hearted serial killer and one of the biggest drug suppliers on the East Coast. He was recently informed by one of his reliable sources that she was planning to go international with her operation. He knew he was the only one who could possibly talk her out of it. Time was of the essence, and he had put all his cartel business to the side to focus more on his legitimate business empire.

Just last week, he held a brunch at one of his private estates just minutes away from Donald Trump's famous Mar-a-Lago estate. The guest list included United States Federal Judge Lavina Armstrong, who was scheduled to sentence him, along with Jason Lewis, the Federal District Attorney. His RICO indictment carried up to a life sentence. Somehow, he agreed to turn himself in and would receive a plea bargain of a year and a day in the Federal Bureau of Corrections for tax evasion and money laundering. His RICO charge would be non-processed due to the District Attorney's office having only a pile of non-circumstantial evidence, coupled with his squeaky clean criminal record and no confidential informants willing to testify against him.

Jah'me also presented each of them with one hundred million dollars, which they gladly accepted. They understood that a case of this magnitude would generate skepticism of bribery from such a wealthy and prominent figure. So collectively, they all decided to wait the full year, after the court proceedings and his release, before any money was to be wired or exchanged. That way, they could be well into their retirement phases without looking suspicious.

Jah'me knew that once he was in the clear with the law, there was nothing he couldn't accomplish legally. Just like he had done running his criminal enterprise. He also wanted to show his sons a healthier lifestyle. How could he preach doing the right thing when he was a cartel boss? He loved his boys and wanted to be a better example for Jah'mille most of all. If it was up to their mother, he would become her personal menace with a gun.

The multimillion-dollar bribe was signed and sealed. Jah'me understood that everything in life came with a price. He was the boss, and he was willing to pay the cost. He took one last shot of his white Hennessy before exiting his helicopter, as his private jet awaited his arrival on the tarmac. He couldn't wait to get back to the comfortable confines of his castle in New Haven, Connecticut.

▼

Baby Cris had been Kandy's lead henchman for more than ten years. He carried out hundreds of hits for her at any given moment. But over the years, he had grown and matured mentally as well as spiritually. He also became a responsible businessman and father. He loved his family and wanted to be present in his son's life. Growing up, he experienced years of abandonment, neglect, and homelessness in the slums of Cape Town. He vowed that he would never allow his son to grow up without the guidance of a loving mother and father.

His relationship with Kandy abruptly went sour when she ordered him to kill a mother and her three children. That was when he knew their partnership had come to an end. He could never kill an innocent child. His newfound pride, principles, and morality just wouldn't allow it. So, without further ado, he called Kandy and told her he was leaving to raise his son and would no longer be working for her. She took his sudden departure as a sign of disrespect. In fact, she called him every name but a child of God and said that if it wasn't for her, his homeless ass would still be on the side of the road eating out of a trash can. Those words pierced his heart, and for the love of Jah'mille and Jah'me, he decided not to kill her.

Unfortunately, Jah'mille sided with his mother, and the two of them had not spoken in over five years. They both understood that if they were ever to see each other again, the love wouldn't be the same. Their cartels had been at war in the United States, and the conflict was now spreading internationally. He didn't see it letting up anytime soon. The problem with Jah'mille was that he didn't ask questions or look for solutions. He killed first and asked questions last. With that in mind, Baby Cris would always keep one eye open. He had taught Jah'mille how to be a stone-cold killer, and now he felt like what he had created could possibly be the death of him. Even though he had grown mentally and spiritually, he was still BC, and everyone knew the count, including Jah'mille.

Had his time expired, or would his hand be forced to kill his best friend?

All he ever wanted was to move his family to Cape Town and live out the rest of his life peacefully while fishing in the Madagascar River.

▼

Jah'mille arrived at his ranch estate in San Antonio, Texas. There sat his elegant hundred-acre waterfront mansion. It was just one of several properties he owned. He entered through a gigantic steel gate with the welded G.I.G. platinum logo on the front of it. Upon entering, he was welcomed by his mile-long driveway, which was lined with foreign and exotic automobiles. His beautiful landscape could be compared to any botanical garden. Some of the rarest sycamore trees and flowers gracefully populated his lawn. Jah'mille called it his Secret Garden.

Ducks, swans, and exotic fish swam the man-made twelve-foot lake, along with a six-foot golden water sprinkler statue of himself.

Five of his top security, several maids, and two butlers all stood outside, lined up awaiting him. It had been several weeks since he last stayed or visited the beautiful estate. As always, his staff was fully prepared for their boss. Jah'mille purchased the property in 2023 when his twin brother Jaylen was drafted in the first round by the Dallas Cowboys. He knew he would be attending his games regularly, so he decided to move there.  The twelve-bedroom, eleven-bath estate was a sight for sore eyes.

Upon entering the lavish property, the twelve-foot bulletproof sliding doors without door handles stopped you dead in your tracks.  Every door was controlled by voice recognition or fingerprint.  His kitchen was enormous and held top-of-the-line, cream-colored appliances, along with cream and caramel matching counters and heated marble floors.  To top it off, he had several golden chandeliers gracing the vaulted ceilings.  This was Jah'mille's refuge whenever he wanted peace of mind.  No one but family, his closest friends, and associates gathered at this particular residence.  He was suddenly surprised and caught off guard when his brother Jaylen approached him.

"What you doing home, fool?" Jaylen asked, also surprised to see Jah'mille.  "The last time I checked, you were back in the motherland," he said, holding a big bag of Lays potato chips.

Jah'mille stood confused.  "The last time I checked, I paid the bills here and I also paid for those chips your big greedy ass is eating up."

"I pay the bills here," Jaylen mimicked him, like he always did whenever he wanted to agitate Jah'mille.

"I don't have time right now.  I see you're in playing mode," Jah'mille replied.

"Man, I just miss my little brother," Jaylen responded, embracing him and rubbing his hand across Jah'mille's head, purposely messing up his waves.

"Man, stop doing that shit.  Why you hating on my 360s, fam?" Jah'mille said, pushing Jaylen away.

"I'm not hating.  I like you without the locks.  You look more approachable."

"But *you* don't with them?" Jah'mille asked, giving him a confused look.

"Of course, I do because I smile more than you, and I play football.  You know all the athletes are sporting locks now.  Plus, I look better than you," Jaylen said, laughing.

Over the years, he'd towered over Jah'mille in height, standing at 6'3" and Jah'mille at 6'1".

"I actually drove over to see if I could borrow some of your drip. I'm attending the NBA All-Star Weekend and I need something exclusive to rock. You know all the big booty girls from around the world will be in attendance, so I needs to be jeweled the hell up. I was just about to text you and ask you for the combination to the walk-in jewelry safe, but look at the universe, my boy," he said, messing up Jah'mille's waves again.

"The combination is always our birthday backwards. You play too much," Jah'mille replied.

"Bro, we do own a jewelry store right up the street for Christ's sake. You're seriously playing right now, "Jah'mille said, walking into the humongous safe, but he knew Jaylen wasn't into jewelry as much as he was. In fact, Jaylen owned a single Rolex and two Cuban link platinum chains.

A blue dimly lit light suddenly appeared. Sparkles glistened from all over. It literally looked like a treasure chest full of diamonds. All Jaylen could see were diamonds shimmering from each individual clear jewelry case. Jah'mille estimated it was well over two hundred million in diamonds alone, not even including the plethora of gold accessories.

"Yes," Jaylen said excitedly, walking around and looking into each glass case. "I want that watch," he said, pointing at the hundred-thousand-dollar platinum and gold Frank Muller. "And I'm rocking all of this right here." He picked up the one-hundred-and-twenty-carat platinum eight-inch Cuban link bracelet and pinky ring set.

"That's definitely going to get you a big booty cutie," Jah'mille said, being facetious.

"I get big booty cuties with my name alone," Jaylen replied, laughing. "But I still need a set of earrings, my boy," he said, walking toward another jewelry case. There sat over twenty-five sets of diamond earrings.

"I want these," Jaylen said, pointing at the one-hundred-carat S1 clarity stones.

In total, Jaylen had just walked out of the safe with over three point five million in jewelry, and Jah'mille acted as if it was nothing.

"I have something I want to chop it up with you about when you return," Jah'mille said, watching as Jaylen entered his new burgundy McLaren with the butterfly doors.

"You did your thing with this one, Jaylen. I haven't seen this make or model in the city yet. How the hell do you start it?" Jah'mille asked, looking inside.

"Oh, it's an app on my iPhone," Jaylen replied.

"That's some ill shit," Jah'mille said, as he watched his brother speed out of the driveway.

He didn't want to be a Debbie Downer and kill the vibe. Jaylen was too hyped about All-Star Weekend. He knew if Jaylen knew how sad he actually was, he wouldn't have even thought about leaving. Just the thought of his father washing his hands of him hurt his soul. The only person besides his mother and brother whom he loved and respected was now gone. He felt that if he were going to make a change, now would be the perfect opportunity.

Of course, he knew his father would always love him, but he also knew that their relationship would never be the same. He walked back toward his garden and sat down by the lake, watching as the ducks and swans swam in circles. He thought about all the great things his father had accomplished, and he truly admired him. He knew that without his father's unconditional love and guidance, he wouldn't have been half the man he was.

▼

Deep down, he felt he had betrayed him which was a feeling he knew too well because BC had been more than a friend to him. He was family. To see him as a rival felt like a hot knife going into his ribs. He had wanted nothing more than to mend what he had tarnished with them both.

Fortunately, he had been wealthy enough to easily leave the streets behind and settle down in Texas with his twin brother. He attended all of his home games. He thought they would just travel the world and date big booty cuties for the remainder of their lives. That was something Jaylen had always reminded him they would do together. Then, he realized that he had never really enjoyed living his life, and it had been unfortunate, because he had everything a man his age could possibly want or desire at the snap of his fingers. He had given *wrong* so many chances, while *right* had stood all alone, pleading to be chosen.

    He noticed how Jaylen lived his life to the fullest and hadn't taken anything seriously. He had been a pillar in the Dallas community. His yearly charitable donations hadn't gone unnoticed. Just recently, he had donated two million dollars to the local Toys for Tots, and every Thanksgiving, he had passed out thousands of turkeys. Jaylen had been loved and adored, and the community respected him.

    Jah'mille realized he was the complete opposite. He never received the love he truly desired, but he received an adrenaline rush when he instilled his wrath of fear. He knew that it had been just Satan himself knocking at his door. It was only a matter of time before his number would be called. His father had always told him that everyone and everything had an expiration date. With the lifestyle he had chosen, he knew that his date would be coming sooner than expected. So, with that being said, he knew he should make the best out of every day. That conversation hit him hard because he knew death was near if he didn't straighten up. He wanted nothing more than to prove his father wrong and to make his family proud of him... for once.

    He was twenty-three years old and had been a juvenile delinquent his entire life into adulthood. He'd made his mind up...he was ready for a change. He decided he was going to seek some form of professional help and try talking to a mental health therapist. He understood he couldn't do this on his own because his mindset was overwhelmed with negativity. Unfortunately, those positive thoughts didn't last long because his mother called...

▼

Jaylen was the talk of the town. Everywhere he went, paparazzi followed and took pictures. Life for him was quite simple since he'd grown up rich. So, whenever his teammates talked about finances, he never indulged. He knew for a fact that he was richer than all of them, and with his father's inheritance, one day he would be richer than the owner. So, those types of conversations didn't interest him.

Even though it was widely rumored that he came from a wealthy family, some said he was the heir to a royal African family. Others said he was the son of a notorious cartel boss, but through it all, he remained positive throughout the chaotic rumors.

Because of this, he asked his family to *dumb it down* a little when arriving at his games, respectfully. Jah'mille would always show up with no less than five security guards and six women. His mother, Kandy, did the most. She always arrived in a ten-car motorcade with five beautiful, gun-toting assistants, along with her personal glam squad and a small army of security. They entered the stadium as if she were the star of the hit show *Housewives of Dallas*.

Jaylen knew that type of attention would place him in the spotlight, but all he wanted to do was play ball. Jah'me would show up too, but he often blended in among the crowd of fans. He knew the Feds were always watching, but nothing was stopping him from the experience. At any given game, he could possibly be in the nosebleed section, sitting alone with his face painted and dressed in Cowboys apparel. No one would ever know. This was another reason why he chose to turn himself in. It tore him apart when he couldn't attend Jaylen's NFL draft ceremony. Events like those were once in a lifetime. If nothing else, he wanted to be able to bask in the glory of his accomplishments as the proud father of an NFL quarterback.

It was two months and fifteen days until he was scheduled to turn himself in to federal authorities. He had so much to do in such a small window of time, but the feeling of finally putting this all behind him was ten steps forward in a positive direction. How could he teach responsibility and accountability to Jah'mille if he was doing the opposite? He Face Timed his best friend, Rob, to give him the rundown.

"Yo!" Jah'me greeted.

"What's good, my boy?" Rob answered with a smile.

"I made up my mind. I'm turning myself in," Jah'me said, straight-faced.

Rob let out a long breath. "I figured that was coming. What you need from me?"

"I'm leaving you in charge while I'm gone."

Rob leaned back. "Say less. You already know I got you. Just tell me Kandy ain't got no say."

Jah'me laughed. "Man, my attorneys already got you locked in. You got power of attorney over my estate. Kandy won't even be able to check the mail."

"Bet," Rob said, nodding. Without another word, he ended the call.

Then, he phoned his pilot.

"Yeah, I'll be flying to Africa in a couple of days. Be ready," he instructed.

Afterward, he called both of his butlers and three of his assistants so they could pack their luggage because they were all headed to the Motherland.

"What's going on, son?" Kandy asked.

"I heard you were back in Texas. Is Jaylen having a home game or something?"

She knew Jah'mille like the back of her hand. He never stayed in Texas unless he was doing business or attending one of his brother's games. To her knowledge, Jaylen was scheduled to attend the NBA All-Star game in Las Vegas the following weekend.

"I needed to get my mind together, so I came here to relax," he said.

"Well, I need you to hurry up and get it together before you arrive in England," she replied.

Jah'mille pulled the phone from his ear, frustrated. Not once did she ask what was on his mind. Kandy always wanted things her way and on her dime. She didn't care about the mental health crisis he was battling or his choice to finally do the right thing for once in his life. He wanted to tell her no so badly, but it already felt like he had lost his father's love and respect. He couldn't afford to lose his mother's too. Even knowing she wasn't right, he still sat there and listened to her devious plan to take over the Westside.

"The first thing I need you to do when you land in England is buy up as many properties as you can on the Westside. Any apartment buildings or homes for sale, mom and pop corner stores, barbershops, car lots, and even clubs. If they're not for sale, make them a generous offer they can't refuse. After a couple of months of construction and renovations, reopen all the storefronts and place our people in position. Once we establish a designated headquarters, we start manufacturing and distributing the product to each location. I'm thinking we fly our workers in once the final shipment is complete." She paused as if she was waiting on his feedback, but he knew he didn't care.

She continued. "A reliable source told me Keshia and Imani are expecting a hostile takeover, but I'm too classy for that. I'm buying up their blocks and stores, upgrading their businesses, and adding value back into the community. Why fight for something you own? As your father would say, *The Art of War* teaches that it's never a physical war when you can outthink your opponent. They're expecting an all-out bloodbath."

"I'm thinking six months from today, we'll be running a string of successful business ventures, stacking English pounds right under their noses. Just in case we need to move aggressively, I'll need you, my adorable son, and your army of rebel soldiers to step in and protect your mother's investment. I can't and won't accept any losses. There'll be no room for negotiations. I want mine back with tax, or in blood." She said it boldly, like she always did. "What do you think, Jah'mille?" she asked.

"It's whatever, Ma. I'm not tripping," he replied.

"Well, I gotta go. I'll call you later," she said before hanging up.

Jah'mille sat in his lush botanical garden, slipping into a deep daydream. He started realizing how blessed his family truly was. They had everything imaginable and more. So, why the hell were they still dealing drugs? Why were they waging war on foreign soil when they were already living peacefully in luxury and royalty? He thought about his father's billion-dollar empire, Jaylen's NFL career, and all the things they had to be grateful for. He just needed to escape his mother's toxic influence. If not, he knew death was waiting for him. He realized long ago it was never about money with Kandy. She reached billionaire status in 2022. It was always about revenge and her twisted need to get back at Keshia for sleeping with his father. She didn't care how many lives were destroyed. The blood on her hands was unreal.

At one point, she struggled with her own mental health but never told anyone except Jaylen and her sister, Courtney. In 2021, her breakup with Jah'me wrecked her. She said it felt like her soul had been ripped from her body. Jah'me was the first man she truly loved. He was the father of her twin sons. He gave her everything a woman could want. He made her laugh and treated her like a queen for over twenty years, but when she found out he slept with Keshia on their 100-million-dollar yacht, she swore to make them both pay. She threatened to divorce him and take half his estate. One night, after a business trip, she accused him of cheating just because he didn't want to make love, and she lost it. She started throwing tantrums, smashing expensive China, and tearing up multimillion-dollar paintings.

Tired of her drama, Jah'me had his attorneys move forward with the divorce. The next evening, while they were having dinner, a FedEx delivery came to the door.

"For a Miss Mendez-Davis," the driver announced.

Kandy signed, and as soon as she handed the pen back, the man said plainly, "You've been served."

She shut herself off from the world for months in her 80-million-dollar Houston mansion. Those were some of the worst times of her life. She lost over a hundred pounds from drinking and drug use. She didn't shower or change clothes for two weeks. Her long, silky hair was matted and tangled, and the bags under her eyes made her look 20 years older. Jaylen and Courtney had to break down her bedroom door just to reach her.

Seeing his mother in that state broke Jah'mille's heart. Seeing the pain on her son's face broke Kandy's. She promised him she would get help. She desperately needed help. Without further ado, she checked herself into the Wellness and Health Clinic for Women in Malibu, California. It was there that she was ultimately diagnosed with depression, PTSD, alcohol, and drug addiction. She remained in their care for six months and fifteen days, learning to love and value herself more each day…mentally, spiritually, and physically.

By her fourth month, her doctors and therapist began seeing positive results. Kandy had returned to her normal weight. At 58, her once-sunken face had filled out, her attractive features returned, and her signature brick house body was back on display. She not only looked beautiful – she felt it. Her overall healing process was rated a total success by the staff, and her stay at the clinic had finally come to an end. Kandy took a moment to personally thank each staff member and doctor for their overwhelming love and support. She was then presented with a certificate of love and self-worth before being officially discharged.

The blazing California heat was different from the dry, humid Houston heat. Dressed in a red Christian Dior blouse, a jean skirt, and six-inch red-bottom stilettos, Kandy exited the Wellness Clinic feeling like a new woman. She was empowered with confidence, self-worth, and a fierce sense that she could take on the world.

She now loved herself unconditionally, so checking into the clinic had been necessary. Not a single family member knew she was there. Kandy was a master at covering her tracks, and she told her assistants that she was going out of the country for business. She used Jaylen's football season, Jah'me's hectic schedule, and sent Jah'mille to London on a time-consuming task to buy herself time. Once a week, she'd do her rounds and check in with everyone.

She instructed her driver to stop at the first KFC he noticed. It had been months since she'd had a crispy piece of fried chicken. The Wellness and Health Clinic catered to a strict healthy diet and didn't serve anything fried. When they pulled up, she noticed the drive-thru was packed. Without hesitation, she stepped out of the Uber and walked inside. The moment she entered, the aroma of fried chicken and mashed potatoes made her stomach growl. Shaking her head in anticipation, she spotted a handsome man sitting alone at a window table, smiling at her. He looked like a cross between a businessman and a younger Nipsey Hussle.

He was dressed business casual, with a neat beard and waves that reminded her of Missy Elliott's famous finger waves. His ring finger was bare, which she appreciated, but she didn't have time for nonsense. Then she looked at his shoes. They were crispy all-white Prada sneakers with no socks. Satisfied with her scan, she smiled back and batted her eyelashes.

He stood and approached. "What's your name?" he asked.

"It's Rachel," she replied smoothly.

"I'm Rick. I'm from South Carolina by way of New York," he said, then motioned for her to join him. He pulled out her chair like a gentleman and asked what she'd like while he walked to the counter.

"As long as it's mashed potatoes and fried chicken, I'm good," she replied with a smile.

Jaylen arrived in Las Vegas around six that evening to his twelfth-floor Presidential Penthouse at Caesars Palace. Sin City was exactly what he expected. Thousands of tourists filled the crowded boardwalk, having the time of their lives. The weather was perfect. It was not too hot or not too chilly after sunset. It was time to drop the tops on the foreigns. He sent four workers from his entourage to retrieve three of his Lamborghinis from the Las Vegas Port Authority. He'd been informed they'd arrived safely, without a scratch.

Jaylen was dressed in Saleem designer, draped in platinum and gold accessories. He was determined to find himself a big booty cutie tonight, either after or during the game.

▼

Back at the KFC, Rick told Kandy he was a businessman and had lived in Houston for over ten years. Kandy wasn't buying it. She'd never heard of him and she knew every major player in and around Houston. That meant one of two things. Either he was lying, or he was just fronting and trying to look the part. Without a word, she began gathering her things.

Rick noticed the change in her demeanor. "Did I do something wrong?" he asked.

She looked him dead in the eyes. "For one, you lied to me. I hate liars."

That statement alone told Rick she was either a boss or had been around one.

"I've never heard of you in the underworld," she said bluntly.

Rick scratched his chin. "Maybe I should've told you my nickname instead. I was trying to approach the conversation in a more mature, diplomatic fashion."

"So, what's your nickname, Rick?" she asked, arms crossed, one brow raised in suspicion.

"They call me Money Man."

Kandy froze. She'd heard that name come up recently, but could never put a face to it. From what she'd been told, Money Man was a heavy hitter. He moved units statewide and internationally. It was also rumored he had a few law enforcement contacts on his payroll. She suddenly saw him as an opportunity. He was someone who could help move her product up and down the East Coast and through the Midwest. She sat back down and re-engaged. This time, she introduced herself properly.

"I'm Kandy," she said.

Rick grinned. "I've never seen you before, but I've definitely heard that name."

After finishing their food, Kandy leaned closer. "Wanna get a hotel room?" she asked.

It had been a long time, and she was more than ready to get her rocks off...

# TWO

**United States Federal Building, Norfolk, VA**

Agents Vick and Cobbs had been the lead federal investigators for over thirty years. Today, they reopened file #1009823, case #098234: *Jah'me Alexander Davis*, a.k.a. *The Black Ghost*. He was believed to be an international drug supplier with ties to cartels in Brazil, the United States, China, and South America. The last confirmed sighting placed him in Cape Town, South Africa. His billionaire and philanthropic status had pulled the wool over the public's eyes. It masked his drug empire and painted him as a savior to urban communities across the nation.

Agent Cobbs took a sip of his coffee. "The only real evidence we had against Jah'me was D.E.A. Agent La 'Marcus Evan aka Zoe. His grand jury testimony would've nailed him. Unfortunately, he was killed in that tragic car crash back in July 2023. His vehicle got crushed like a soda can after being hit head-on by a semi... just weeks before he was scheduled to testify."

Agent Vick chuckled. "Man, you know damn well Jah'me ordered that hit."

"Oh, for sure," Cobbs replied, flipping through the case file. "The problem is proving it. It looks like Jah'me's taken a back seat the last few years, letting others run his operation. Somehow, federal records show he only got sentenced to a *year and a day* in the FBC for money laundering and tax evasion." He slammed the file shut. "That's a sweetheart deal for a man who's a prime RICO candidate."

"This isn't what I signed up for," Cobbs muttered.

"This case stinks of collusion. Somebody's getting paid off. Let's take a deeper look at District Attorney Jason Lewis and Judge Lavana Armstrong. They both had to approve those plea deal terms. I want their recent financial records—CDs, domestic and international bank transfers, the works."

"I'm on it," Agent Vick replied. "If we find anything, Jah'me won't be the only one doing federal time."

▼

**Sunset Boulevard, Los Angeles**

Green, yellow, and black Lamborghinis cruised bumper to bumper down the congested Sunset Strip. Jaylen rode shotgun in the green Lambo, butterfly doors up.
His entourage was flanked by motorcycle police escorts. People watched in awe, some recognizing him as the Dallas Cowboys' star quarterback, others simply dazzled by the flashy cars and glimmering jewelry.

When they arrived at the basketball arena, Jaylen noticed a group of attractive women waiting in line to enter. He sauntered over and introduced himself, inviting them to join him in his VIP skybox. They giggled, exchanged glances, and happily accepted. The box was decked out. There was catered, gourmet food, music, champagne, and a panoramic view of the court. Jaylen's attention gravitated toward the shortest of the bunch, Channel, a Dallas native. She was about 5'4", curvy, with a bright Colgate smile and a body that turned heads.

"I thought you'd be a complete ass like most celebrities," she said playfully. "But you're not. I noticed how you made sure everyone here was treated with respect. That means a lot."

Jaylen chuckled, humbled. "You're too kind," he replied. "And honestly, all this jewelry? I borrowed it from my brother. Had to put on for All-Star Weekend."

Channel laughed. She loved his honesty and energy, but she didn't know that this version of Jaylen was new even to himself. They excused themselves to the hallway for privacy and were flanked by security as they talked for nearly an hour. Jaylen asked if he could see her again in Dallas.

She hesitated, then admitted, "I'm actually sleeping on a friend's couch. Just broke up with my abusive ex. My girl won five tickets to the All-Star Weekend in a local talent show, so she brought me along. I've got a hundred dollars and a plane ticket left to my name." She smiled softly. "This whole experience has been a blessing. Thank you…for everything."

Jaylen was moved. "You didn't ask for anything. That says a lot."

She joked, "Once I get on my feet, I owe you a sexy steak dinner. Just give me a few months."

"I'll hold you to that," he grinned.

They returned to the suite where goodbyes were exchanged. Jaylen and Channel kissed passionately, his hands tracing her curves.

"I guess I'll be calling you when I get back to Dallas," she whispered.

"You *guess*?" Jaylen teased, slipping her two thick wads of cash.

She blinked in shock. It had to be over $10,000.

"I'm looking forward to that steak," he said with a wink.

"I promise it won't be long," she replied, kissing him one last time before they parted ways.

As Jaylen entered his black Lamborghini, teammate Raequan shook his head.

"How much was that?"

"A light twenty racks," Jaylen said, smirking. "That steak better be good." Jaylen said, entering his black Lamborghini and driving away down Sunset Blvd.

▼

Jah'mille was enjoying a relaxing day at his ranch estate for the very first time since purchasing it two years ago. Today, he toured the twelve bedrooms and eleven bathrooms, property, and basked in the sun while feeding bread to the ducks and swans for about an hour. Afterward, he retreated inside to watch *Kevin Hart: Laugh My Heart Out* in his private home theater. His day was far from over. After smoking a few blunts with his twin maids, the trio decided to play strip poker in the man cave.

Jah'mille considered the Texas ranch the ultimate vacation getaway. It was a peaceful place of solace – something he desperately needed. He eased into the jacuzzi with the twins, who were taking turns washing different parts of his body while he puffed his marijuana and watched the UConn Lady Huskies take on Notre Dame. It had been a long time since he'd simply sat down and enjoyed a game.

Wanting complete privacy, he turned off all communication devices and instructed his assistants to notify him only if Jaylen called. He was taking his mother's advice and embracing what she used to call "me time." After a hot, relaxing sponge bath, he took the show on the road. They headed straight to his elegant master bedroom. There, he received a full-body massage with hot coconut oil while sage candles and blueberry marijuana smoke drifted through the air. Rihanna's *Wild Thoughts* played throughout the surround sound system as both Spanish bombshells danced naked atop his dresser in six-inch red bottoms. Jah'mille was living his best life. He recorded the twins dancing and sent the video to his brother with the caption: **"Big Booty Cutie Alert!"**

Pulling the shorter twin onto his California king mattress, they began an unfiltered sexcapade, while the other continued dancing seductively. Just then, his phone lit up. It was a message from Jaylen.

> **You know they really think you're me, right? lol. I BEEN told you Brianna and Bella were freaks. Glad to see you finally enjoying yourself, fool. I'll catch you in a few days. Out here in Vegas trickin' up a lil change.**

Jah'mille chuckled. Lately, Jaylen had been living it up. He was traveling the world and spending cash. With a five-year, $68 million football contract, plus new sneaker, State Farm, and Gatorade endorsement deals, he could afford it. Not to mention his $300 million inheritance. If he stayed consistent, Jaylen would hit billionaire status before turning the age of 40.

As for Jah'mille, he was already worth $200 million, with investments stretching across the U.S. and internationally. In Cape Town alone, he owned multiple thriving businesses. His mind felt clearer now that he was staying away from Kandy and her chaotic world. Could he actually leave the cartel and run a legitimate empire? His father would be proud... but what about his mother?

That was the ultimate question. Still, the decision was his to make. He'd come to love his solitude. So, for the next few weeks, he went off the grid, laying low at his San Antonio estate. There, he practiced self-care and nourished his mind, body, and spirit. He fasted and prayed five times a day. It was time he took accountability for his thoughts, actions, and decisions. Time to become the righteous man he knew he could be.

▼

**Three Weeks Later...**

Jah'me, Rob, Jaylen, and his team of lawyers arrived at the United States Federal Jail in Norfolk, Virginia, at 7:00 a.m. sharp. Jah'me wore jeans and a simple T-shirt. As soon as they entered, several armed agents stood waiting, alongside the two stooges themselves, Agent Vick and Agent Cobbs. The second he stepped through the door, they pounced, searching and cuffing him. Jah'me gave Rob a calm nod. Jaylen stepped in for a quick hug before he was taken away.

Rob knew that feeling too well. Though his own arrest had happened over twenty years ago, he could never forget the cold grip of steel cuffs digging into his wrists or the icy six-by-twelve cell he'd called home while fighting his case. Still, he knew Jah'me was built different. He could handle anything because he was cool, poised, and professional. Rob also believed this was a necessary move for his friend's growth. Jah'me's billionaire status and philanthropy had always been clouded by suspicion. No matter the good he did, he couldn't escape his past. He couldn't attend awards, banquets, or public events. Now, finally, he was stepping up and owning his truth. Even though, deep down, they all knew... the feds had nothing.

Jah'me sat alone in his cell for thirty minutes until he heard the heavy steel door unlock. Several agents stood staring at him like they were seeing an exotic animal in a zoo.

"Is it really him?" one asked.

Agent Vick stepped forward. "It's definitely him. Back from the grave. Jah'me Alexander Davis, aka *The Black Ghost.*"

The 150 million dollars was wired to an offshore account in Belize to a high-ranking customs agent named Anthony Bailey. Allegedly, he controlled the shipments on the docks down at JFK. Keshia had Montano pay fifty million, and Imani had Ceaser pay the other hundred million. That way, none of the shipment would get confiscated or have to be tossed into the ocean if, or when, the Coast Guard showed up.

Imani had been taking shipment loss after loss for the past several months, so Keshia understood why she was hesitant to proceed. Except, just as any cartel jefe would say, you have to pay to play. Any other way, you would have taken a major loss in the drug game. The ten metric tons was enough cocaine and heroin to supply the entire England for a couple of months and, by their estimation, would bring in over 30 billion dollars in street value alone.

Imani couldn't believe this was actually about to happen. In total, this was the biggest shipment she had ever been a part of. She and Baby Chris were back at their estate eating dinner when she brought up the shipment.

"Baby Chris!"

"What's up?" he replied. He was watching the soccer game on television.

"Our ten metric ton shipment is due to be en route to England," she said excitedly.

Baby Chris didn't even seem fazed. As of late, he was starting to fade away from the street life, and unfortunately, it seemed as if she was getting deeper into it.

"Can I be honest with you?" he asked.

"Of course, baby," she replied.

"You know that all good things eventually come to an end, right? And that everyone and everything has an expiration date?"

"Okay, I'm lost, Jah'me," she replied, being facetious, knowing exactly who he learned that quote from.

"I guess what I'm trying to say is, I feel like this cartel lifestyle has finally played itself out. What's new, baby? It sure isn't the money, because we have enough of it to last us three lifetimes. I just want to be able to enjoy it with my beautiful family. It's like the more money we make, the bigger the risk we take on. I feel as if I've put in enough work, just as well as you have, but when will enough be enough? I just want to be a good example to our son and raise him to be a respectable man. I want him to be the total opposite of how I came up. So, with that being said, after this shipment, I'm strongly considering being done with the drug game."

Words like that would have normally made any wife or mother cry with tears of joy, but not Imani. She stood and quietly listened. After, she replied that she was happily married to an amazing man and the father of her handsome son. He was her best friend and confidant, but she was also married to the dope game.

"When you met me, I wasn't a housewife, I was a hustler. Baby Chris, I didn't choose this lifestyle. The lifestyle chose me. No matter if I decide to stop hustling today, tomorrow, or even next year, I'm internationally known and will forever be targeted and investigated by the Feds as the Queen of Cocaine. So with that being said, I'm going to ball out until I fucking fall out...with or without you."

Without another word being said, she exited the living room and left Baby Chris stuck in his thoughts.

▼

Rick thought he knew Kandy, but he had no idea. For hours, they talked and made business plans. Kandy learned and verified through her contacts that Rick could, in fact, transport heavy shipments and had connections down at TSA and with U.S. Customs and Border agents down in El Paso, Texas. She desperately needed this connect. The drugs were easily available. It was transporting and smuggling them that was always a challenge.

Rick somehow found the nerve to almost question if she could afford his services. "We're talking multi-millions of dollars!" he reminded her.

Kandy found his comments to be quite offensive, but she knew he didn't know any better. She tried her best not to put too much thought into it. As long as they came up with a solid business agreement, she was cool. The remainder of the night, they engaged in consensual sex.

The following morning, Kandy's flight was scheduled to depart around 7 am, and Rick's flight was scheduled around 9 am. A loud knock at the door startled them both. Rick jumped up and looked out the window.

"Oh shit!!! Looks like the Feds are outside!"

"The Feds?" Kandy said, looking confused. She walked to the window and peeked. That's when she noticed it was her Cadillac motorcade. She quickly got dressed and opened the door. Rick looked as if he'd just dropped a load in his pants.

"Come on, I guess I can drop you off in Texas."

He couldn't believe that a ten-Cadillac truck motorcade was there to pick up one woman.

They arrived at the airstrip and boarded her private Learjet. Within a matter of minutes, they were ascending three thousand feet in the air and eating breakfast while reading the newspaper. Rick looked over at Kandy getting her hair and makeup done by her team of assistants. That's when he knew that she was the real deal. She knew exactly what he was thinking, too...*with his green ass*, she thought.

▼

Jaylen was punch drunk seeing his father getting detained, but he understood and knew it was only temporary. He declined to talk to the media as he rushed out of the jailhouse with Rob by his side. Once they entered their vehicle, Rob looked at him and said, "Today is the start of a new beginning for your father and our family. It's only up from here, nephew!"

"No doubt," Jaylen agreed, looking out the window at the chaotic media presence outside the jail and the hundreds of onlookers crowding the sidewalk all hoping to get a glimpse of the drug lord.

Unfortunately for them, he had arrived at seven instead of eight and wouldn't be transported until the FBI motorcade and police helicopter were in place. Jah'me was still considered one of the most powerful men on the planet. Even though he had voluntarily turned himself in, the Feds still had to move with serious security precautions.

▼

Imani felt horrible after her conversation with Baby Chris. She talked Keshia's head off the entire night while sipping on her favorite bottle of Bella Bollé Pink Moscato. Keshia knew the feeling all too well. She wanted out of the game at one point herself, but she knew she'd signed her life away the moment she picked up the phone and called Montano back. Same for Imani. There was absolutely no way Jefe Ceaser would ever let her leave La' Familia. He had already agreed to let her sister, Sage, go several years ago. Now that Imani was earning his cartel billions in revenue, leaving unscathed was damn near impossible. Still, Keshia listened and tried to lighten the conversation.

"Baby Chris is changing for the better, Imani," Keshia said. "I remember like it was yesterday when you were complaining about him never being home. And now that he's less active in the streets and more present, you're the one that's always gone."

"But I be out getting to that Birkin, sis!" Imani shot back.

"Girl, boo! And he wasn't?"

"Baby Chris *is* the bag!" Keshia replied. "I know he's worth a few hundred million, and between both of your incomes, y'all could fly away in one of those Lear jets, buy a remote island somewhere off the grid, and live your lives to the fullest. Away from all this nonsense."

"Don't tempt me," Imani replied, laughing. "I was thinking, after we secure this billion-dollar shipment, maybe I could link back up with Jah'me," Imani said. "Ask if he'd strongly consider talking to both Jefes for both of us."

"You think it'll work?" Keshia asked.

"It wouldn't hurt to try," Imani replied.

Imani had one ace of clubs in her spades hand. She knew for a fact that Baby Chris had a strong father-son bond with Jah'me. She also knew Jah'me, Ceaser, and Montano were all close business associates.

▼

Rob was hosting his annual banquet for young, up-and-coming Black entrepreneurs in Los Angeles. Thanks to LA's infamous bumper-to-bumper traffic, Jaylen arrived at the Staples Center two hours late. Fortunately, he still caught Rob's closing speech. Jaylen stood backstage as Rob captivated the sold-out crowd of over career-minded Black men and women with an inspiring, motivational message.

"Here's the truth. Every human being has genius-level talent. There are no chosen ones. You just have to find what you're great at and tap into it. Just know that on your journey to success, nobody's going to believe in you until you've already done it. Nobody's going to celebrate with you until you've already done it. The work in the battlefield has to come before the belief. That means you're going to have to put in work, for a *long time*, by yourself. No applause, no rewards, and nobody pushing for your success. But stay committed, because without commitment, you'll never start. Without consistency, you'll never finish. Last, but not least, *ease* is a greater threat to progress than hardship.

Every teaching institution teaches history. But I bet you've never heard of a future class. That's because they want your mindset stuck in the past. Meanwhile, the world you're living in is evolving and advancing daily. Stay woke. Keep grinding. Keep growing and evolving, mentally, physically, and spiritually. But most importantly, through it all, stay positive and I'll see you all on the battlefield."

The crowd rose to its feet in a standing ovation. This was just one of many stops Rob made throughout the year. It was his way of giving back, teaching financial freedom, and educating his people on generational wealth. It was something he and his siblings were never taught growing up.

His philanthropy extended far beyond his banquets and speeches. Despite his packed schedule, every dollar earned from his events was donated to inner-city youth programs and the Black Lives Matter organization. Hs donations alone topped two million dollars that year.

Rob exited the arena with Jaylen, flanked by security. He told Jaylen that he had tried calling Jah'mille several times, but the phone kept going to voicemail. He wanted to let him know about his father. Jaylen replied that he planned to tell Jah'mille, but not just yet. He explained that Jah'mille didn't want to be bothered and had decided to step away from the streets for a while and lay low.

"Is everything okay?" Rob asked.

Jaylen nodded and began describing how Jah'mille was transitioning into a healthier, more positive mindset.

Rob burst out laughing, but he quickly realized Jaylen wasn't joking.

"So, you're serious?" Rob asked.

"Without a doubt," Jaylen said. "For the past few weeks, he's been off the grid. That's something unheard of when it comes to him. But like my father used to say, 'in order to be something you've never been, you have to do things you've never done.' Jah'mille's been working on himself mentally, physically, and spiritually. I've been checking in on him, and I believe this is his season of transition."

"That's amazing to hear. Jah'mille's intelligence is through the roof," Rob said. "We could definitely use a mind like his out here on this battlefield of success. Let him know I'm proud of him whenever you see him."

"You already know I will, Unk," Jaylen replied.

Rob knew Jaylen would never give up his brother's location. Their love and loyalty ran deep to the grave. After arriving at LAX International Airport, the two embraced. Rob was headed to Jah'me's headquarters in Cape Town, South Africa. Jaylen was flying out to join his brother in Texas. He boarded his private jet and within minutes, he was asleep before takeoff. It had been a long, hectic day and an even longer flight ahead.

It had been three weeks, and Kandy still hadn't gotten back in contact with Jah'mille. All Jaylen kept telling her was that he'd heard he was okay. Without further delay, Kandy decided to handle the things Jah'mille normally would've taken care of. His absence was completely uncharacteristic, but she was determined not to let anyone...especially Jah'mille...interfere with her money train.

She met back up with Rick at an undisclosed location. Dressed in an expensive Hermès hoodie and jean outfit, her designer shades covered the cold determination in her eyes.

Rick entered her Cadillac, and without a minute to spare, Kandy cut to the chase.

"So... is the operation a go or not?" she asked.

Rick assured her that his people were making the proper adjustments for the massive shipment.

"Just let me know the numbers," Kandy said. "My time is money, and every day, hour, minute, down to the second, I'm losing it. Rick, I'm not comfortable using that L word."

"I understand, Kandy. I'm going to get directly down on my people at JFK. I know it's been chaotic lately with Trump imposing tariffs on Mexico and China, so a lot of container shipments have been stalled or never shipped at all. It's backing up the system. It's not that I couldn't ship containers. We just can't get to them. It's like a needle in a haystack of containers at this point. It depends on what products are being exported with them, and when they're scheduled for arrival."

Kandy didn't want to believe him, but she was highly in tune with current events, especially politics, so she could understand why things might be moving slower. Still, the fact that her five containers full of cocaine were now sitting ducks, made her blood boil. It was a massive liability. She excused herself and stepped out of the SUV. Rick noticed she made a phone call using a black phone, not her usual pink iPhone with the glittered case. That's when it clicked...she had two phones. Nine times out of ten, that black phone was a burner she used to call Jah'mille. After a few minutes, she returned to the vehicle and told Rick they'd reconvene in a week. By then, customs and TSA should have cleared out more of the backlog.

  Meanwhile, in Colorado, Jah'me arrived at ADX Florence, a twelve-story underground supermax prison in the middle of the desert. It housed the most dangerous criminals known to the FBI, CIA, and DEA. Although he was only charged with tax evasion and money laundering, his federal custody level placed him in this level-six maximum-security prison. To the feds, Jah'me was still one of the most powerful and dangerous men on the planet. Five hours outside of Colorado, this escape-proof, 24-and-1 lockdown facility was home to El Chapo, Ted Bundy, the Unabomber, the surviving Haitian pirates who hijacked the *Maersk Alabama*, and one of the Arab terrorists from 9/11.

  Privacy didn't exist.

  His cell had no window, no radio, and no television. It was just him and his Qur'an. He was allowed one hour a day outside his 9-by-12 cell. It was just enough time to stretch his legs, shower, and make a quick phone call. Even though that wasn't simple at ADX Florence because calls were made in a tiny room with a wall phone and three chairs. Two were occupied by correctional officers who not only listened but also took notes during every call. Jah'me realized if this was how he had to communicate, he wouldn't be using the phone system at all.

  The food was awful, and his mattress felt like a concrete slab. He wouldn't wish this place on his worst enemy. This was going to test him mentally, physically, and spiritually.
It was his *universal test*. It was a time for knowledge, wisdom, understanding, and growth. They could lock up his body, but his mind...his mind was free. With time and discipline, he knew

his creative genius would rise again with a new blueprint for financial freedom and generational wealth. For now, he laid back on his slab of a bed and began counting the cracks in the ceiling until his eyes grew tired.

▼

Back in Cape Town, South Africa, Rob sat at Jah'me's luxurious multi-billion-dollar headquarters. He'd been waiting to hear from the Boss for days.
He understood the legitimate business plans and protocols. His main focus was keeping the operation running smoothly. He knew Jah'me ran an international drug empire, but figured someone else had been left in charge of that side of the business. Running Jah'me's company was no small task and it showed how much faith and trust Jah'me had placed in Rob. With over 300 employees, 10 lawyers, six assistants, five accountants, and an army of armed security guards, Jah'me operated like a Fortune 500 CEO. Call after call, proposal after proposal, billion-dollar deals poured onto Rob's desk, and he was already feeling overwhelmed. He reflected on a conversation he and Jah'me had years ago, while sitting in the back of his Maybach.

"If anything ever happens to me," Jah'me had said, "I want you to take over my company."

Jah', you know I hate when you start talking like that," Rob replied.

"I know, brother. But shit happens and you're the only adult I trust. Just make sure my boys are straight."

"Without a doubt!" Rob said. "But Jah', I wouldn't even know where to start. Running a company this big? I can't even see how you're doing it."

"Yes, you do," Jah'me replied. "All you gotta do... is think like me."

Rob had never forgotten those words. In a way, that moment was the motivation he needed now more than ever. He turned to his assistant.

"Bring me my coffee," he said.

Then he rolled up his sleeves and got to work, sorting through the mountain of proposals and invoices stacked on his desk.

▼

**Jah'mille's Texas Estate...**

"You sure you want to do this?" Jah'mille asked, laughing as he held a pair of hair trimmers above Jaylen's head.

"Hell yeah! I'm proud to be the big brother of a renewed and changed man. You inspire me, fool."

"Well, don't be too inspired yet," Jah'mille joked. "I still got a couple of people on my hit list."

He was flattered that Jaylen wanted to cut his dreads so they could look alike. Jah'mille had only cut his off because he'd been going back and forth to court, and the dreads just weren't a good look anymore.

"You still not gonna have waves as sweet as mine, fool. This takes hard work and effort," Jah'mille said, glancing in the mirror while brushing his waves forward.

"Man, we share the same DNA. If you can get 'em, then so can I. So I'm not even trippin'," Jaylen replied.

It had been fifteen years and six months of having dreadlocks, and now they were completely gone. The first thing Jaylen said after his haircut was how much lighter his head felt. Jah'mille agreed and called one of his maids to clean up the mess.

Living on his Texas ranch had been surreal. He could have never imagined living so peacefully in the confines of his own estate. He was finally enjoying life. He'd attended five of Jaylen's football games, several Houston Rockets games, and even toured San Antonio for the first time. His newfound freedom was priceless, because he understood he wasn't just changing for himself.

**Coverdale, England**

Keshia sat inside her 20 million-dollar mansion, thinking about the possibilities. Something about this last shipment had spooked her, but she knew she needed it. Still deep in the hole after Montano fronted her $300 million, she desperately needed this lick. At a time when they should've been celebrating, she and Imani were planning their escape from both their cartels instead. She knew that she couldn't ask Jah'me for a favor of that magnitude because of everything he was dealing with.

After locking in the one shipment with Imani, she began working on her next one. She always had a backup plan for her backup plan. Looking down at her phone, she noticed a missed call from Money Man. He'd left a message telling her to get back with him ASAP, and time was ticking.

**Downtown Dallas...**

Channel's condo sat in the heart of Dallas, just ten miles away from Jerry's World. Today, she was expecting a visit from Jaylen for the first time since she'd moved in. They'd talked on the phone several times, but both of their schedules had been hectic. Today, they were finally catching up. Wearing her tight Jaylen Davis jersey dress and a pair of leather, knee-high boots, Channel was more than excited to see him again.

Jaylen pulled up around 7:30, driving his matte blue two-tone bulletproof Lamborghini truck. He was dressed in a blue and white Polo shirt, blue denim shorts, Versace designer sunglasses, a Polo bucket hat, and a pair of crispy all-white Air Force Ones with no socks.

"Oh my, you're lookin' right handsome," Channel said, looking him up and down. "But... there's something different about you."

Jaylen grinned and stood silently for a moment, waiting to see if she'd notice. Then, he took off his bucket hat, revealing his fresh haircut.

"You cut off your dreads?"

"Yeah, had my brother cut 'em earlier today."

"If I may add, I think you look a *lot* better without them," she said, winking.

"Thanks," he replied. "You look and smell amazing too. And I'm definitely feelin' that jersey dress."

"Oh, thank you!" she said, tugging playfully at the fabric. "He's my favorite player."

"What position does he play?" Jaylen teased.

"Quarterback!" she said confidently.

"Okay," Jaylen chuckled. "I see you been watchin' me."

"Of course!" she said. "I haven't missed a Cowboys game since we met."

Jaylen felt like he had his very own personal cheerleader. He really liked Channel. She was good people and genuine to the core. Her aura and energy were infectious. That energy had drawn him in from the beginning, and the fact that she was an official big-booty cutie. She gave him a tour of her two-story luxury condo. Jaylen loved it. Each room was painted and decorated differently, with its own unique elegance. He loved it so much that he asked if she'd decorate his new townhouse, and she gladly agreed.

After the tour, they walked hand in hand down her glass spiral staircase into the dining room. A beautiful candlelit setup awaited them. The first thing Jaylen noticed was the two bottles of Ace of Spades chilling in an ice bucket. There was also a vibrant fruit platter with strawberries, watermelon, pears, blueberries, bananas, and peaches. Soothing R&B sounds from October London played softly in the background. Jaylen popped the cork on the champagne while Channel stepped into the kitchen. She returned moments later carrying an amazing steak and potato dinner, complete with sweetened lemon iced tea and a strawberry cake for dessert. She sat across from him, watching as he took his first bite.

Jaylen bowed his head, said grace, and prayed the steak was delicious. He had been looking forward to this day for over five months, and now it was finally here. Channel didn't disappoint. Her steak was so tender and juicy that it melted in his mouth. It was seasoned to perfection. He didn't have to say a word because his expression said it all.

For the rest of the evening, they talked about love, family, finances, commitment, and most of all, children. With the last bottle of champagne and the fruit platter in hand, they eventually retreated to her master bedroom for an unforgettable nightcap.

▼

Rick worked for the United States Customs division in Miami, back in the early two thousands. He was a dedicated Lieutenant Major, working in the shipping department for over ten years. His job was to oversee the entire operation by making sure he kept other countries and the United States' port authority safe from as much criminal activity and drugs imported and exported, foreign and domestic, as much as possible. He really was a no-nonsense, zero-tolerance supervisor who was often known to police his own workers.

Knowing the temptation was always present, he didn't allow anything to get past him with his keen eye and professional experience. He was given several awards, and the Mayor of Dade County had recently presented him with a key to the city, after he methodically orchestrated the bust of a shipping container coming in from China with over a billion dollars of fentanyl. It was enough to kill the entire United States population. Rick took pride in what he did. He literally lived and breathed justice, police reform, and border security.

One early summer morning, he exited his Dade County residence on his way to work when he was suddenly approached by several men. Panic set in, and before he could reach for his service weapon, he was gun butted in the back of his head and instantly knocked out. He was awakened several hours later, after being drenched with a bucket of ice-cold water, soaking his entire body. There stood an attractive young black woman dressed in an all-white pantsuit. The group of men stood alongside her, masked up, dressed in police issued army fatigues, and holding AR-15 assault weapons.

She began talking without an introduction. She went on to inform him why she was there in the first place. She said that his team of customs agents seized several of her shipping containers. It was estimated to be in the billions.

So, he had two options from this point on, and his first option was that he could die right now. She began laughing at the scared face he'd just made. His second option was that he could live, but he would be indebted to La' Familia for the remainder of his natural life. She thought to remind him that his beautiful family were all going to die first. She began to tell him the story of his life, and from what he heard, it was nothing or no one she didn't know about.

His daughter, Gianna, was a freshman at Penn State, and his son, Derrick, was the starting quarterback for Norfolk State University. She also told him about his secret affair and the child he just had with his secret wife. She knew all about the double life he was living, and promised that none of them would see another Christmas if it was up to her, but the choice was his to make. In all, she knew she had him by the balls. Rick looked up in defeat and said he would do whatever was needed. Imani smiled and told him that he made a smart decision.

**Nine Months Later...**

Rick was under investigation. The DEA and FBI were all in on the bust. From their records, it looked as if the majority of the red-flagged overseas containers were making it into the port. They realized it was because most of the drugs were getting seized on land through weigh stations and random vehicle searches. His confiscation numbers over the years had drastically decreased. So, the Feds and the DEA secured a warrant to execute their raid the following morning. Rick was informed about a suspicious container shipment coming in. When the shipment arrived, he had his custom agents reroute it and replace it with a container designated for Walmart. Minutes later, his office was raided, he was detained, and put on administrative leave without pay.

**Five Years Later...**

Rick was finally released from federal custody. As he walked out, one thing was clear...he still had an obligation to La' Familia. He didn't waste a minute. He knew they knew exactly when he'd be released. At the first gas station he could find, he used the track phone number they'd given him. A woman answered, and he recognized her voice instantly.

"How does it feel to be free?" she asked.

"It depends," he replied.

She laughed. "I'm not going to put any pressure on you, Rick. You're part of the team now." She asked for his location and told him someone would be there to pick him up within the hour.

Two hours passed, and finally, a black Cadillac Escalade pulled into the lot. Rick walked up and climbed inside. The driver handed him an iPhone.

"Press 1. Then, hit send," the driver said.

Rick did.

Imani answered on the third ring.

"I'm overseas in London," she told him. "Won't be back in the States for another two weeks. But I need you to know that we need you. Your knowledge of port authority and customs is more valuable than ever." Then she said, "Open the briefcase behind you."

Rick reached for it, popped it open, and saw it packed with stacks of hundred-dollar bills.

"That's your coming home present," Imani said. "The truck, the driver...it's all yours. There's also a fully furnished townhouse waiting for you in Houston." She continued, "Your task until I return is simple. Recruit some of the customs officers you still have ties with at the port authority. Offer them each a million dollars. If they don't bite... well, you already know what the second option is." She laughed. "Why do people have to make things so difficult?" she sighed.

"Oh, and one more thing. You need to change your name. It has to stick. It needs to be something that tells them exactly who you are. My goal is to make you the connection. You would be the man for drugs and transportation in the criminal underworld. You busted your ass for customs, and look how they treated you. That's $300,000 just for you to enjoy," she said. "Don't save it. Don't stash it. Spend it. Hit the clubs, the car shows, the events. Let 'em know we have the product. I just need you to network. Put your name out there. Make noise. Before you know it, they'll be calling you The Money Man."

# **THREE**

  The twins were together in Los Angeles for the first time in years. Jaylen was no stranger to the big city lights and cameras. He'd been the poster boy for his Division One alma mater, the Alabama Crimson Tide, for three years. He had starred in Gatorade, Nike, and State Farm commercials and made a host of guest appearances on daytime television.
  "Just follow my lead, bro. They're gonna ask you a couple of questions, but it's mainly sports talk," Jaylen said, reassuring his brother.
  "I can handle it," Jah'mille replied, excitedly. He remembered watching *SportsCenter* with their father as a kid and had been a huge fan since the Stuart Scott days. Small microphones were pinned to the collars of their Tom Ford designer suits. Jah'mille immediately recognized the host, Stephen A. Smith. They shook hands before both brothers embraced Molly. Jah'mille always thought she looked good on TV, but in person, she was breathtaking. The show's producer approached, counting down.
  "We're going live in five... four... three... two... one."
  "Good morning, and welcome back to another edition of *SportsCenter*! We've got two very special guests in the building today. None other than the number one player in the nation, Heisman Trophy recipient, NFL's 2024 Rookie of the Year, and starting quarterback for the Dallas Cowboys..." Stephen A. paused for dramatic effect. "...Jaylen Davis, along with his twin brother, Jah'mille! Welcome to the show, fellas! I'm loving the Tom Ford double-breasted suits. Y'all looking sharp. Can't hide that money!" Stephen A. said, approving of their expensive attire.

"Thank you for having us," they said in unison.

"Let's get right into it and talk football. Your team, the Dallas Cowboys, are having yet another disappointing season. No playoffs... again. Even with all those trades and max deals, y'all still came up short. Can you tell me why? *Why* didn't you go out and get Saquon 'The Rocket' Barkley? The boy's having a sensational season. Box office stuff. Dallas, being one of the wealthiest organizations in the league, didn't even glance his way."

"Injuries, Stephen A.," Jaylen replied. "Not being able to keep a healthy roster is a problem for any team. I just play the game. That question's for our owner and GM, but yeah, I agree. We could've used someone explosive like Saquon and a few more defensive linemen to help out Micah Parsons. Still, I'm confident we can make it work with what we've got."

"Only if you can keep Coach Jerry off the field," Molly interjected.

The entire panel burst into laughter.

"The Dallas Cowboys are taking the fun out of football," Stephen A. shot back. "They stink! Yeah...injuries... sure, but let's be honest, they still would've folded before the playoffs. There's a black cat haunting your franchise! No championship any time soon!"

"And Jah'mille," Molly turned, "Who's your favorite team?"

"I'm a New Orleans Saints fan to the grave," Jah'mille said proudly.

"And that's exactly where they're headed!" Stephen A. hollered.

"The Saints stink too! Four and nine! They've got an all-world defense, but their offense? One of the worst in the NFL, especially in the red zone. Two straight seasons under .500. Let's get it together, Saints!"

"Well, Stephen A., in our defense, we've got injuries, too. Trading Lattimore didn't help. Firing our head coach? That was the last straw. Honestly, I think we should've hired Bill Belichick," Jah'mille replied.

"The Saints haven't been a powerhouse since the Drew Brees era," Stephen A. said. "Still, they're always fun to watch."

"Before we let you go...Super Bowl predictions?"

"Kansas City Chiefs and the Philadelphia Eagles," Jah'mille said.

"Buffalo Bills and the Detroit Lions," Jaylen added.

"Well, thank y'all for stopping by. Come back and see us again!" Stephen A. said.

"I most definitely will," Jaylen replied.

They wrapped up the interview with Stephen A. and said their goodbyes.

"That was a dream come true," Jah'mille said, grinning from ear to ear.

They were in the back of Jaylen's Maybach, watching the taping of the show on YouTube as they headed to Jaylen's mansion in Baldwin Hills. Jah'mille was finally living his life to the fullest. It felt amazing to be happy for a change. He knew he'd eventually need to face Kandy, but this time, if she tried to drag him back into his old ways, he'd cut her water off without hesitation. He was finally learning to love himself more than he loved his mother, and he knew there was nothing wrong with that, now.

This was Jah'mille's first time at Jaylen's estate, which his brother had purchased over five years ago. Jah'mille was in awe of how alike they really were...not just in looks, but in taste. Jaylen's L.A. estate was a $44 million marvel. It sat on five acres, eight bedrooms, seven bathrooms, a six-car garage, a man cave, an indoor pool, and a home movie theater. Jah'mille could tell Jaylen spent a lot of time there. Unlike himself, Jaylen was settled and content. Jaylen had recently bought a townhouse in Dallas since his job was there. Before that, he'd either flown private back and forth or stayed in hotels. Tired of living out of a suitcase, he finally settled down and had his new boo, Chanelle, interior decorating the place while he was away.

Jaylen had big plans for the next morning. He was taking Jah'mille out on his private yacht for a fishing trip. It would be their first time ever going together. For some reason, Jaylen felt an urgent need to spend as much time with his twin as he possibly could.

▼

Keshia and Imani were eating at one of Keshia's soul food restaurant locations in Chesapeake, Virginia. It was yet another packed house. The food was so amazing that people traveled from different states just to enjoy some of her finest cuisine and live entertainment. Keshia's Country Kitchen was more than just a soul food spot. It was an all-out dining experience. She only hired the best chefs and grill masters coming out of culinary arts school, and she paid them exceptionally well. She believed in putting love into everything you do, so she only hired people who thought and believed the same. On the back of each employee's shirt read:

**"We cook your food with love, so you're eating experience remains the same."**

Her five-star rating and record-breaking sales proved it. Even with three locations throughout the city, you still had to make reservations. It was never a day where Keshia's Country Cooking didn't cater to a packed house. She welcomed walk-ins as well, but only after 8 pm until closing at 10pm.

*"Gurl! These collards are slamming, ya' hear me?"* Imani said with a mouthful.

"*Yes!!* The barbecue chicken, ribs, and this baked mac and cheese…a missile!"

"So, what's been going on at the home front?" Keshia asked.

Imani swallowed her food and went on to explain that she and Baby Chris just weren't seeing eye to eye anymore.

"He's on some *back to Africa* shit, girl! I'm so through with him. I told him my son not going to no damn Africa. I don't care if he's treated like Prince Hakeem. He's not taking my baby! Did I ever tell you about the time he kidnapped me and flew me all the way to Cape Town?"

"No!" Keshia replied, leaning in. "I need to hear this tea."

"It happened way back when I was first introduced to Jah'me. We were flying on one of his Lear jets. It felt like we were in the air for a day. When we finally landed on the tarmac, Baby Chris pointed toward this white Rolls-Royce. I exited the Lear and entered the vehicle. That's when I noticed my connect, Caesar, sitting inside. He introduced me to Jah'me. That's how I met him."

"More like kidnapped you to Jah'me," Keshia said, laughing. "Jah'me and I had a light fling. He was so laid back and cool, it was ridiculous. I desperately needed him to keep Kandy off my top. I owed her 30 million at the time. We went in together on a few business ventures, and a month later, she wanted payments. She was being super petty and started harassing me every other day. My back was against the wall, so I visited Jah'me and told him about her constant threats. He shook his head and, instantly, he wrote me a check. It was enough to pay her off and still have a quarter-million left for myself. I was so grateful to finally get her out of my bag."

"So, he just wrote you a thirty million, two hundred and fifty thousand dollar check, out of the blue?" Imani asked.

"Just like it was thirty-two hundred dollars, girl! He told me to stop dealing with her. I hugged him tightly and...surprisingly...he kissed my neck and palmed the hell out of my ass... for what felt like minutes. Then, he told me to get with him later. I automatically knew what that meant. I was like, Yesss daddy! You know Jah'me love him a big ass!"

They both burst out laughing. Imani sat in shock, mouth wide open.

"I arrived at his yacht a week later, dressed in my *come-and-get-it* skirt with no panties and my sexy heels. He explained that, yes, he wanted to hit this big ass, but he also needed to take some pictures of us having sex and that he'd block out my face. I said I was game and instantly got naked."

"Was he working with something?" Imani asked.

"Gurll!! He was hung like a German racehorse," Keshia said.

"I know that's right!" Imani yelled, accidentally alerting the customers sitting nearby.

"He said his plan was to get his freak on, get his money back, and make his exit from Kandy."

"Did his plan work?" Imani asked.

"From what I know about Jah'me, all his plans seem to work themselves out. I'm pretty sure he got his money back. I know for sure he got his nut," Keshia winked.

"You crazy," Imani said, shaking her head.

"But enough of the small talk. What's the word on the shipment?" Keshia asked.

"I heard back from Rick yesterday. He informed me that we successfully intercepted Kandy's five containers, but only four are en route as we speak from JFK to Miami-Dade's Port Authority. I have my customs agents waiting on-site and at the weigh stations. We've got seven eighteen-wheelers ready to roll."

"Is there any way Kandy can link this lick back to us?" Keshia asked.

"The only link is Rick," Imani said, sipping her tea.

"Should we kill him as soon as the shipment secures the docks in Miami?" Keshia asked.

"It would be the typical thing to do," Imani replied. "But... he's a part of La' Familia now. Once we reroute the shipment, we distribute and supply the bricks to as many states and clients as possible. We make a clean run and pay off Montano, with interest. I'm thinking a billion should free you, sis," Imani said. "Still leaves us with half a billy each, and that's after everybody's palms get greased." Then, her tone changed.

"But I'd be lying if I said I wasn't nervous. Kandy is one of the most ruthless, cold-hearted motherfuckers I've ever met in my life," Imani added. "She has *no* cut card. All she seems to know now is killing. Staying completely under her radar is mandatory," she warned. "I'm also setting up a police sting operation down at JFK. The minute Rick informs me Kandy has arrived, customs agents will execute a raid on the one container we left behind. We'll make sure she sees it happen. After her arrest, she'll be told that all *five* containers were confiscated by the DEA. If everything works out, Kandy's ass will be locked up and we'll be back up again. Rick is aware of the possibility of getting arrested along with Kandy," Imani said. "But I'll do everything I can to get him out..."

The jet landed at Boulder International Private Airport. Jaylen and Jah'mille stepped off the aircraft and entered a black Cadillac Escalade.

"Where the hell are you taking me, bro?" Jah'mille asked.

"It's a surprise," Jaylen said, smirking. "Just be patient, fool."

The Colorado Rocky Mountains were a sight for sore eyes. The beautiful scenery reminded Jah'mille of a Christmas postcard. The weather was cold and frigid, crisp enough to bite.

After driving for over fifty miles, Jah'mille noticed they were approaching a secured area. Several signs flashed past, but one in particular made his stomach drop:

**ADX Florence Supermax Prison**

"Jaylen, what the hell is this? I know you not bringing me to a damn prison. You know I got warrants!" Jah'mille said, raising his voice.

"You're gonna be alright, bro. I've already got you covered. They don't even do statewide background checks. They only check felonies committed in Colorado."

"That's... weird," Jah'mille said, still eyeing the gates.

"It's facts. I wouldn't risk your freedom. You already know that," Jaylen replied calmly.

"By the way, who the hell is so important that we traveled this far just to see them?" Jah'mille asked.

"You'll just have to wait and see."

Inside the Prison, Jah'me had been expecting his sons' visit, even though he'd told Jaylen several times not to come, but he knew Jaylen wasn't trying to hear that. The screening process was standard. Jaylen breezed through and went to complete paperwork for both of them while Jah'mille was being searched. When Jah'mille finally stepped out, he spotted Jaylen standing nearby and holding the papers with a suspicious look on his face.

"You not slick!" Jah'mille said, eyeing him. "I already know it's either Poochie or Ayone locked up in here. This bitch a max, too. My nucca probably put that steel in somebody. But I'm leaning more toward Poochie though..."

They entered the visiting room and sat for what felt like forever. Jaylen's celebrity status had everyone distracted. The CO's gathered around asking him for autographs and selfies. They thanked him and wished him a good visit.

Suddenly, a side door opened and out walked Jah'me, dressed in a beige prison jumpsuit and orange slides. He looked through his gold Chanel frames, his waves spinning, and his million-dollar smile lighting up the room. Time seemed to stop. Jah'mille froze in place. Was it the spice he smoked earlier, or was that really his father standing right in front of him? Heartbreak and reality hit instantly. Jah'mille had no idea his father was incarcerated. Jah'me wrapped his arms around both his sons. The hug lasted minutes, but felt like forever. Tears streamed down Jah'mille's face. They were real, ugly, crocodile tears. Jaylen wiped his own eyes because he was unable to hold them back.

"Get it together, son," Jah'me said gently. "Everything's going to be okay."

"But how? When?" Jah'mille asked, voice shaking. "You're on the FBI's most wanted list..."

"They didn't come for me. I turned myself in," Jah'me said. "It was a decision I had to make for my growth and for yours. How can I tell you to do the right thing when I'm out here running from the law?"

"For how long?" Jah'mille asked.

"A year and a day," Jah'me replied. "Just like I told you back at the courthouse in Cape Town...nobody's untouchable. That only exists in the movies. Our family's empire has surpassed every obstacle stacked against black men. We've become what the Rothschilds, Rockefellers, and Carnegies were to white wealth. The Davis family is royalty, and our legacy will be written in the books...economics, real estate, business... generations will know our name. So, where does your name sit now at the royal table?" Jah'me continued.

"Because Rob is running the empire back at headquarters, and it should be one of you in that seat. There's no victory without sacrifice, son. That's universal law. But this time will pass. I'll grow mentally, physically, and spiritually. You should, too. I've heard great things about you. Your brother said you've been ten toes down, staying out of the chaos, and doing right. I was floored. Couldn't believe it at first, but I know exactly when it happened...the day I told you I washed my hands of you, right?"

Jah'mille nodded with his head low.

"I knew you had greatness in you, son. I had to be the sacrificial lamb to bring it out."

"But Pops... how did you get a bid that short? One year and a day?" Jah'mille asked.

"When you put in the legwork, it gives you leverage. If I was gonna do time, I was doing it *my* way."

"That's gangsta," Jah'mille said, shaking his head, clearly impressed.

Jaylen and Jah'me both laughed at his comment.

"I'm not turning back for shit... excuse my language, Pops," Jah'mille added. "That's just how serious I am about change. Not just for me, but for the family. I want to do it my way, too."

"You're already on the path, whether you see it or not," Jah'me said. "I mean, I don't ever remember you letting Jaylen take you anywhere without your wrecking crew."

"I've learned that when you're doing the right thing, you don't have to look over your shoulder," Jah'mille replied.

"No doubt," Jah'me said, nodding. "So, what's the plan for the rest of the day?" he asked.

"We'll probably just settle in for the night and fly out in the morning," Jaylen said.

"See, Pops?" Jah'mille grinned. "This man's celebrity status turned him into a tender dick. We can sleep on the jet! I'm trying to find us some good weed and a couple big-booty cuties. Pops, this fool in love already?"

Jah'me just sat back, watching his sons talk, and smiled.

Baby Chris was back at his and Imani's luxury Chesapeake estate with their son, Christopher. Together, they'd had a fun-filled day riding in the back of his Maybach, sightseeing, and soaking in the beauty of the Seven Cities. Earlier that evening, they played a game of pickup basketball at Norfolk City Park. After about an hour, they headed to Greenbrier Mall in Chesapeake, where Baby Chris bought several PlayStation games and three pairs of Air Jordans for his son. They walked around, ate ice cream, and then drove to the Virginia Marine Science Museum in Virginia Beach. Christopher really enjoyed the experience and asked if they could return next time with his mom.

"Without a doubt," Baby Chris said, reassuring him.

They planned to play PlayStation and eat Marco's Pizza for the rest of the night. Baby Chris sat down beside his son and rubbed his head. He smiled as he looked at him, but Christopher was locked into the PlayStation game. He resembled Imani so much that it was crazy.

"Son, how would you feel if I left to go back and live in Africa?" Baby Chris asked.

Christopher looked up and said, "Why so far, Dad?"

"Because it's my home. It's where I feel most comfortable, but if you tell me not to go, then I won't."

At just 10 years old, Christopher was highly intelligent. He knew his father loved him, but he also knew how much he missed home. Baby Chris talked about Africa constantly, and Christopher had recently overheard an argument between his parents about taking him there.

"I wouldn't mind you leaving," Christopher said, "as long as you came to visit me."

"Oh, I'd always come visit. Maybe, in time, you can fly out to Africa and spend a couple of weeks with me. We can go Air Jordan and game shopping again."

"Sounds like a plan," Christopher replied, high-fiving his father without even looking away from *Call of Duty*.

That conversation gave Baby Chris the confidence he needed to finally make his move. He had come to terms with the fact that things were over between him and Imani. They'd become more like distant roommates than lovers. He had grown out of the life, while she still clung to the street glory. Still, no matter what, he'd always be there for her just not as her man.

▼

Meanwhile, Rick and Kandy arrived at the Port Authority right on schedule. Kandy stepped out of the vehicle dressed down in Dior red tights, a black and red Dior hoodie, red, black, and white Air Max 95s, and her signature Chanel designer sunglasses. The dock was crowded, so they blended right in.

Rick approached the dock supervisor, who also happened to be a U.S. Customs agent, and the two shook hands. The agent led Rick and Kandy down the dock until they reached their container. He cut the seal with a pair of bolt cutters and cracked the door just enough for Kandy to peek inside. It was packed to capacity. You couldn't fit a banana in there if you tried.

The agent took out a test kit and sliced a small hole in one of the bricks, It was just enough to get a sample. Within seconds, the clear solution turned dark blue and confirmed it was cocaine. Kandy shook the agent's hand and walked back to her vehicle with Rick, but she never got the chance to drive off. Within minutes, their truck was surrounded by DEA and FBI agents with AR-15s drawn and aimed.

Kandy burst out laughing. "Okay, so this was a setup the whole time, huh?" She turned to Rick and added, "You better pray I don't find out you're a fuckin' rat."

Rick looked her dead in the eyes. "I was just thinking the same thing about you." Then, he calmly stepped out of the vehicle with his hands in the air.

▼

Back at the estate, Imani walked in and saw Baby Chris and Christopher asleep on the couch. She headed upstairs to the master bedroom where she immediately noticed something was off. Most of Baby Chris's belongings were missing. She glanced toward the door and saw his luggage sitting nearby. Not wanting to entertain the thought, she opted for a long, hot shower instead. It had been a stressful day. An hour later, she stepped out and found Baby Chris standing in the center of their bedroom floor, naked.

It had been a long time since they had even kissed, but for some reason, she didn't resist. She dropped her robe, revealing her naked body, and walked over to the bed. Baby Chris came up behind her, kissing and caressing her. Before they knew it, they were making love, wordlessly, all night. Nothing was said because everything was understood. The next morning, Imani woke from a deep sleep and reached across the bed.

Baby Chris was gone.

His side was empty, and his luggage had disappeared. Reality hit that he had left for good, but without him watching her every move, she could finally focus on what she loved most...getting money for La' Familia. Baby Chris was already in the air, headed back to Cape Town on his private Lear jet. This time, he promised himself that he would never leave again.

Jaylen and Jah'mille arrived back in Texas around two in the afternoon. Jaylen had a Monday night game at Jerry's World against the New Orleans Saints. He asked Jah'mille if he planned on attending.

"I wouldn't miss seeing my boys kick ass for the world. It's not that often I get to root against you," he replied.

On the way back, Jaylen had his chauffeur drop him off at practice and handed Jah'mille the keys to his townhouse.

Jah'mille noticed that Jaylen lived in a secluded neighborhood. Judging by the luxury cars, it was obvious most of the football players lived there. It was a convenient 10-minute drive to Jerry's World, so it made perfect sense.

Upon entering, Jah'mille was taken aback by the décor. The high Baltic ceilings and huge fireplaces were breathtaking. The beige marble kitchen and appliances probably cost more than the townhouse itself. Andy Warhol's expensive art pieces graced the walls. Overall, Jah'mille wasn't surprised. He was just impressed, but right now, he wanted nothing more than a hot shower and some good rest. The long trip to and from Colorado and seeing his father had drained all his energy.

After a long, hot shower, Jah'mille checked his phone and noticed Jaylen had texted saying he'd be home later. He decided to smoke a fat blunt. He laid on the bed and played Lil Baby's "California Breeze," several times before falling into a deep sleep. He was suddenly awakened by a dark-skinned woman standing directly in front of him, completely naked, and dancing seductively to the R&B song "Birthday Sex" playing in the background.

*What the hell was in that weed?* he thought, looking at the leftover roach in the ashtray. The woman was every bit of 5'4", 150 pounds of pure thickness, and to top it off, she was gorgeous.

"I'm not Jaylen, I'm Jah'mille!" he yelled over the music. That was the first thing that popped into his head. He noticed she had a wine bottle in her left hand and could tell she'd already been drinking.

"And I'm not Channel, I'm Ciara, baby," she replied, squeezing her breasts and winding her hips.

He laughed, figuring she was intoxicated.

The name Channel sounded way too familiar. He jumped up, covered her with his blanket, and quickly got dressed. Something told him this was Jaylen's girlfriend, but hadn't Jaylen told Channel about him? He left the room and called his brother, leaving "Ciara" naked and clueless.

Jaylen entered the house and noticed Jah'mille was alone.

"Where's Channel?"

"I'on know," Jah'mille replied. "I guess she got embarrassed and left after finding out I wasn't you. I told her she was good, though. I definitely wasn't tripping. Real spill. She lucky, though. You know the old Jah'mille would've had her lil' thick ass folded up like a pretzel on that cute little sofa in your living room."

Jaylen chuckled and called Channel. He knew his brother like the back of his hand, and he was right. The Jah'mille he'd always known didn't have a cut card and was freaked all the way out. For him to do what he said he did, and with Channel confirming, it showed growth and a willingness to change.

Channel arrived back at the house 30 minutes later. Jaylen hugged her the moment she walked in and assured her he wasn't upset. Together, they walked to the kitchen where Jah'mille was sitting at the table, eating cereal out of a gigantic fruit bowl. Jaylen reintroduced them again, and they all burst out laughing the moment they met eyes.

"It's amazing how much you two resemble each other," Channel said.

"Yeah, we know. Been hearing it our entire life," Jah'mille replied.

"The only difference I notice is the height. Other than that, you look exactly like each other's clone," she said, shaking her head in disbelief.

Kandy was in the bullpen plotting her next move. She had a bad feeling about Rick all along. He wasn't moving like a true shipper. She'd dealt with more than one in her career as a cartel boss. She was going to get to the bottom of everything, but for now, she needed to get out of jail. Her all-star team of lawyers was already working on securing her bond. She demanded they have her out within the hour.

Courtney Aaliyah Mendez, the mayor of San Antonio, was also Kandy's younger sister. The moment she heard about Kandy's incarceration, she had several government officials dispatched to Rikers Island, where Kandy was being held.

Kandy was charged with CCE–Continuing a Criminal Enterprise–and first-degree international drug smuggling. After being debriefed by federal agents, she was given back her phone, jewelry, and released through the back door into the custody of Texas officials.

Rick, on the other hand, was released through the front. He claimed he was forced to work for Kandy and feared for his life. Federal agents didn't believe half of what he was saying. But they knew Kandy's reach and the power she held. He was told he'd have to testify before the grand jury against her. He was placed in protective custody.

Agent Vick had Kandy's phone tapped and was now the lead investigator on her case. He felt he'd fumbled the rock with Jah'me, but not this time. He had evidence piled high and was determined to bury Kandy and her associates under the prison

Imani got the call from one of her reliable court officials. She was already on the phone with Keshia when she clicked over to take the call.

"Damn, he snitched?" Keshia asked.

"He better had. He didn't have a choice. It was either he worked for her or me. He knows his position in La' Familia, and he's playing it quite well," Imani replied, puffing on a blunt. Now, let's get back to business. The way things are looking, you'll be out of Montano's pockets in no time," Imani said.

Back in Cape Town, Rob was running Jah'me's empire like a well-oiled machine. Everything was operating smoothly. After reviewing the revenue and capital gains in several of Jah'me's accounts, Rob realized it was nearly impossible for them to lose. Jah'me was doing in business exactly what he used to do in the drug underworld, but instead of flipping metric tons across the globe, he was flipping real estate and building construction marvels.

Rob was stunned after receiving a three billion loan from their partners at the France International Bank to build a soccer stadium in Italy. After crunching the numbers with Jah'me's six accountants, they estimated that it would cost Davis Building Industries $1.5 billion to construct. After paying every employee and repaying the bank's minimum monthly payment of $100,000, the company would still come out $800 million in the green, with $100 million of that reinvested into the company.

Rob immediately began construction on the new Davis Shopping Outlet Mall just minutes away from the stadium. The accountants agreed that it was a brilliant investment and expected to generate millions in revenue in its first quarter. Major outlet brands such as Nike, Gucci, Prada, Tiffany, and Rolex were already lined up to join. Contract negotiations and construction developments like these were piled onto Rob's desk daily. Jah'me had mastered the art of using other people's money to create wealth while letting his profits make even more money. It was knowledge Jah'me had drilled into Rob for years. Rob never imagined how much that guidance would transform him professionally. Even though the accountants handled 98% of the work, he stood over their shoulders, watched, asked questions, and learned. He was fully committed to growing this powerful empire, his best friend had built from the ground up. Rob had just experienced his first real taste of financial freedom and the staggering reality of generational wealth. All made possible by Jah'me's billion-dollar blueprint.

▼

Meanwhile, Jah'mille couldn't go any longer without checking in with his mother. Even though Jaylen was keeping them both updated regularly, it just wasn't the same. Kandy never told Jaylen the full truth, especially about her street life. Jah'mille understood she was trying to protect him the same way he wished she had protected him.

"It is what it is," he muttered to himself, staring at his iPhone. He finally felt strong enough to talk to her. His father taught him he was only responsible for his own thoughts, ways, and actions...not Kandy's. So, with that in mind, he dialed her number.

"Jah'mille!!! Boy, I'm going to ring your damn neck when I get my hands on you! Where the hell have you been?" Kandy screamed. "My ass been to jail and everything. You were nowhere to be found!"

Jah'mille sat quietly and let her rant. It was something she often did to make him feel guilty, but not this time. He'd prepared for this moment.

"I need you, son. Where are you?" she asked.

"First of all, I called to tell you that I love and miss you. I was hoping to hear the same," he replied calmly.

She noticed something was different in his tone, but couldn't quite place it.

"Jah'mille, I been telling you I love you your whole life. Come on now, you killing me with this soft shit all of a sudden."

"Ma, I'm not getting involved," he replied. "I can come see you, but my peace of mind means more to me."

"I know this nucca ain't talking about peace of mind! You done drove a bitch crazy for 23 chaotic years, and now that I really need you, you want peace of mind? Jah'mille?!"

She hung up on him.

He felt hurt for a moment, but then remembered what his father once told him...*Growth hurts, because not everyone will grow with you.*

He knew he was all that Kandy had left. Maybe his absence would finally trigger a change in her, too. She would never put Jaylen through what she put him through. So, why him?

As he thought about Jaylen, his phone vibrated.

"What's up, fool?" Jah'mille answered.

"Cooling out. I just finished practice. You coming over for dinner?"

"I'm not hungry, bro. I'm just gonna kick back and watch SportsCenter talk about the Cowboys all damn day."

"And you know it," Jaylen replied, immediately picking up on his brother's energy.

Without another word, he made a U-turn at the next light and headed to Jah'mille's estate.

It had been two months and twelve days since Agent Vick tapped Kandy's phone. Now, the federal investigation was officially an open case. Jah'mille was wanted in the United States for conspiracy to commit murder. If the conversation he just had with Kandy was considered legitimate evidence, he could be charged again.

His father, Jah'me, had secured him diplomatic immunity, as long as he stayed on African soil, but Agent Vick's data showed the call was placed to a number located in Texas. Vick needed confirmation before filing for an arrest warrant. He knew how common Google numbers were in the criminal underworld, and Kandy wasn't dumb enough to talk openly over a regular line. Vick spent the rest of the day calling multiple phone companies because he was determined to verify the numbers.

# **FOUR**

C-62 Section B, Cell 13 was where Jah'me would be held for the next twelve months. There were no windows or signs of life. It was just four solid brick walls and complete silence, all day, every day. No TVs. No radios. All Jah'me heard was the cold, frigid air blowing hard from the ventilation system, the toilets flushing, and the opening and closing of the large steel cell doors slamming shut. It actually felt warmer outside than it did inside the prison.

Jah'me's legal team had informed him that the facility pumped in freezing air during winter to keep inmates in bed and calm. Even the correctional officers walked around in bomber jackets, scarves, hats, and gloves. He realized this prison was built for mental warfare and designed to break people. It would've driven most men insane, but not him. They could trap his body, but not his mind. His mindset stayed sharp and full of focus and positivity.

Jah'me started his day at 5 am, saying his prayers, meditating, and thanking the universe for his physical health as well as his spiritual and mental wealth. After the five-thirty headcount, he knocked out two hundred burpees, two hundred push-ups, and a hundred squats. Staying active was not just for his health, but to keep his body temperature up in the early hours. He was allowed to order *Black Enterprise* magazine, which featured Black entrepreneurs, innovators, and billionaires. He also subscribed to the *Colorado Chronicle* newspaper. Over hot coffee and his favorite chewy chocolate chip granola bars, he studied the Nasdaq and Dow Jones, checked his daily shares and stock reports, and took notes on new IPOs that piqued his interest.

Sticky notes with motivational quotes were taped all over his wall. One of his favorites read:

**"The first step to accumulating wealth is being willing to do today what others won't, so you can have tomorrow what others can't."**

He read that quote every single day. He understood that nothing was handed out and everything had to be earned. He could've been under the covers like ninety percent of the inmates at Florence, but he wanted more. He was taught that the worst time spent was wasted time. It took hard work and determination to become a billionaire and even more to remain one.

▼

Back in Cape Town, Baby Chris arrived at his exclusive 10-bedroom villa. He was greeted by his live-in butler. After an hour of walking around, smoking a blunt, and thinking, he realized the estate was far too big for just him. He told his assistant to put it on the market immediately. Driving into the city, he noticed the newly built one-bedroom condominiums just five minutes from the airport. He made a mental note to check them out later. Cape Town, South Africa, was on the rise. Jobs and business opportunities were blossoming for the youth, and Baby Chris was determined to give back to the same community he once terrorized.

If anyone could shift the youth's mindset, it was him. He'd made hundreds of millions doing the wrong things. At only 25 years old, he still felt unfulfilled and as if his real purpose hadn't yet revealed itself. Before he left the States, he told Imani he planned to do something meaningful with his money. He never mentioned the exact amount until after their RECENT breakup. That's when he told her he planned to donate over one hundred million dollars to African youth organizations.

Imani had assumed a light million, tops. When he told her the real figure, she lost it. They shared a Swiss bank account. She felt blindsided, like he was using the donation to spite her. She snapped, told him to go to hell, and hung up on him. The following week, Chris called back to let her know, out of respect, that the withdrawal would be happening soon. That's when Imani said she was flying in. She wanted a face-to-face conversation. He didn't understand why, but he agreed anyway. His mind was made up. There was nothing she could say to change it.

Imani felt Chris was overstepping. The money may have been there, but it wasn't all his. She had invested in that account, too. Together, they had bought homes, jets, jewelry, and luxury cars all from that one shared fund. Now, he wanted to drain a chunk of it for a cause she didn't approve of? Absolutely not! She wasn't about to let it slide. She made up her mind that she wasn't leaving Africa until they figured this out.

▼

Meanwhile, Jaylen had heard about Jah'mille's recent phone conversation and couldn't have been prouder. His little brother had finally stood up for himself. That was something Jah'mille hardly did when it came to Kandy. He was always the first to jump when she called. Not this time. This time, he was firm on living life on his own terms. Jaylen had traveled the world and experienced so much, but seeing his brother finally at peace meant more than anything. It meant more even more to him than his own draft day. All he ever wanted was for Jah'mille to be happy and truly live, and it looked like he finally was.

They hugged for a long moment. Jaylen told him how proud he was. Even in that happiness, Jaylen knew one thing, and that was his brother was still a wanted man in the States. The longer he stayed, the more he risked his newly claimed freedom. It was time for Jah'mille to head back to Cape Town where his diplomatic immunity still protected him. Jaylen wasn't about to let anything jeopardize that.

Agent Vick received a fax from the FBI and was informed that both phone numbers were not burner phones and were still active. His only dilemma was that he couldn't secure a warrant from Apple to search either iPhone, but all hope wasn't lost. He was still able to use his international phone-pinging system to locate both devices. He had already served indictments on Rachel Mendez, and Jah'me Davis had finally been apprehended and put where he belonged. Now, if only he could bring in their certified hitman, and son, Jah'mille Davis.

"I can probably roll the dice that his plea bargain will be no less than a life-plus sentence, but of course, we're shooting for the death penalty," he said, speaking to his new partner, Agent Angela Mackie, a ten-year police captain out of the Norfolk District. She could still remember when the Rude Boys terrorized the Tidewater area.

"That man had over twenty bodies before he was even eighteen. And guess what, Mackie?"

"What?" she replied.

"The crooked African government spit right in the face of the American justice system by granting him full diplomatic immunity as long as he stayed on African soil."

"That's unbelievable!" Mackie responded. "But how?"

"His father is a billionaire. He's like the freakin' mayor of Cape Town. The man owns forty-eight percent of the city's real estate. As cops, we're allowed to be wrong and make mistake after mistake," Vick continued. "But as a felon on the run, one mistake could be your last." He glanced down at Jah'mille's case file. "I have strong reason to believe our suspect, Jah'mille Davis, has given up his diplomatic immunity and has been living under the umbrella of the U.S. government this whole time. Think about it. Why wouldn't he? The rest of his family is already living here."

*Agent Cobbs is probably turning in his grave right now*, Vick thought to himself. Cobbs had just passed away shortly after Jah'me turned himself in.

"Thirty-four years chasing this ruthless family," Vick said, holding up an old photo of him and Agent Cobbs. "And it's almost three for three. This was us back when we raided Jah'me's first mansion in Virginia Beach, over thirty years ago."

"Damn, he's been rich that long?" Mackie asked, studying the photo and case file. "He looks so young."

"It says here he was born in 1974. That makes him fifty in 2024."

"Yeah, he's been flying under the radar for decades. We didn't even know what he looked like until after our twenty-first year of investigating, but we always believed he existed... even when the evidence said otherwise. We always knew we were right." He added. "We're making it three for three. We're bringing in Jah'mille. Justice for Agent Cobbs."

"For Agent Cobbs," Mackie agreed, high-fiving him.

They both grabbed their jackets and headed out of the precinct.

▼

Imani's plane landed at Mandela International Airport around noon. Before heading to Baby Chris's mansion, she made a stop in the slums of Kingston. She knew a couple of thugs there and needed their assistance.

Cape Town had changed drastically. It had been over 10 years since her last visit, and the city was thriving. With its new developments and high-rise buildings, it was starting to resemble Charlotte, North Carolina. She finally saw what Baby Chris had been trying to show her all along. He'd told her she'd like it, but the truth was, she loved it. Still, she just prayed he could understand her perspective. She had risked her life and freedom for the money in that joint account... the same money he was now planning to donate to an organization he'd never even heard of.

When her Uber pulled up to his estate, the first thing she noticed was the "For Sale" sign on the lawn.

"Damn! He's selling the estate, too? I put in on this house as well." She stormed through the glass doors, yelling, "Baby Chris!"

"Hold it down! What's your problem?" he asked, looking confused.

"You the damn problem! How you gonna sell the estate without asking me if I agreed to it or not?"

"Because I bought it with my money," he replied, already irritated.

"I gave you five million on it," she shot back.

"And I put a 10 million dollar ring on your damn finger, so what?" he snapped.

His eyes were bloodshot from stress and marijuana.

"You taking from me because I'm a woman, huh?" Imani said, standing with her hands on her hips.

"Did you come all the way to Africa to harass me? You starting to act like your idol, Kandy. No loyalty or morals. It's sad when you put money and drugs before your own damn family."

"You acting like you a damn saint, BC!" she yelled. "The ice-cold killer talking about morals? You done turned into Creflo Dollar overnight!"

"People change. I'm done with La' Familia. Our son means more to me than this material shit and the glamorized drug life you're so obsessed with."

"You a clown," she spat.

He laughed, and she took it as disrespect.

She slapped Baby Chris. He reacted by slapping her back. She hit the floor hard, her nose bleeding. She pulled a gun.

He reached for it, and she fired. The bullet hit him in the chest. They struggled. He got the gun and shot her in the stomach. Bleeding heavily, Baby Chris slumped to the floor. Imani lay next to him, barely breathing.

"Damn... so this how we going out, huh?" she whispered, tears falling as she watched him fade to black.

Heartbroken, she watched until finally, she slumped over too and stopped breathing.

▼

Kandy was scheduled to turn herself in to the United States Federal Courthouse on Monticello Avenue the following Monday morning before 9 am, but by all means, that wasn't happening. Even though her sister Courtney had pulled a few strings to get her out on bond, there was just no way Kandy could see herself living in a dirty-ass cell ever again.

She loved and respected her sister's political position, but it wasn't like Courtney did it for free. Not at all. It was only after Kandy had her assistant deliver two million in cash to Courtney's front doorstep that things started moving. That's when Courtney finally got off her ass and began the process of getting her bond approved. So, like it or not, Kandy felt that Courtney could kiss her ass.

    With over a hundred and twenty Louis bags stacked outside of her Learjet, she called Jah'mille's phone, as well as Jaylen's, before leaving for Africa. Jah'mille answered once, and their conversation lasted five minutes. It was just long enough for Agent Vick to ping the call in Dallas, Texas. With that lead, he contacted the Dallas–Fort Worth Fugitive Apprehension Team to inform them of a wanted fugitive taking refuge in their city. He was working on getting a warrant signed by a judge and sent over the suspected address for surveillance until he arrived. Agent Vick then faxed a photo of Jah'mille. After ending the call, he and Agent Mackie exited the precinct and headed straight to the United States Courthouse.

    Meanwhile, Rick was ducked off, living off the grid in Green Bay, Wisconsin, under a federally mandated, court-ordered protective custody agreement. It was there that he learned, from an inside source, that Imani and Baby Chris had both been found deceased in Cape Town, South Africa. He felt like an elephant had been lifted off his shoulders..like his life had just made a 180 in his favor.

    He knew Imani's entire operation inside and out. Every pickup time, date, location, and who he was expected to collect money from.

    "This can't be real," he said, pacing back and forth in his apartment. He knew this shipment alone would bring in over a billion in profit. His only concern now was Keshia and if she knew the full extent of the operation. From his recollection, she only helped fund it. If that was the case, she'd be clueless about the move he was about to make.

Keshia was heartbroken in more ways than one when she heard the tragic news. Imani and Baby Chris were both dead. South African authorities stated it was a fatal love-suicide-homicide. The police on the scene reported the butler's statement. He said he had only witnessed the couple arguing. He claimed he quickly dismissed himself and stepped outside to tend to the vehicles. Not even five minutes passed before he heard two gunshots, he said. He rushed back inside to find them both lying on the floor, bleeding profusely. Before he could even dial for help, he noticed both had stopped breathing. He checked their pulses... nothing. He also stated the gun found on the scene did not belong to his employer, Mr. Christopher Rogers.

Keshia hadn't known the actual logistics of their operation. Only Rick and Imani knew the pickup and drop-off locations. She stood in the center of her 28 million-dollar mansion and bawled up in tears. She couldn't win for losing. How could they fumble the billion-dollar bag at the one-yard line? This drug game was an endless trip to destruction. There were no winners, but there were two outcomes...death or prison.

Keshia had everything she could ever imagine. Still, she wanted more. That was the poison of the drug game. It turned dealers into addicts for money the same way crackheads were addicted to drugs. In the end, it all ended the same way.

Scared for her life, Keshia knew the infamous Kandy was still at large and had reliable inside sources. Government officials, FBI agents, and judges were on Kandy's payroll. Keshia feared her name would surface soon just by association. She and Imani had been thick as thieves for over five years. She got down on her knees and prayed that God would forgive her and deliver her from this lifestyle. She grabbed the Bible her mother had gifted her just last Christmas and opened it for the very first time. A bookmark was already placed inside, with highlighted words that read:

**"What profits a man to gain the world, and to lose his soul?"**

That verse pierced her soul. She had everything a woman could want, yet she was still unhappy. Life was simpler and better before the riches and the cartel. She knew she had to change, and she was willing to make that sacrifice, even without the money she owed Montano. Keshia was determined to leave the game on her own terms. If she were to die, it would be a righteous death. She prayed for grace and forgiveness.

▼

The autopsy report somehow made it to Agent Vick's desk. It showed blunt force trauma to Imani Davis's head and a single gunshot wound to her lower abdomen that caused her to bleed out. Christopher Rogers suffered a single gunshot wound to the right side of his chest that resulted in a collapsed lung.

"This has to be one of the best days of my damn life," Agent Vick said, grinning. "Putting knotty-headed scumbags in the grave or under the jail never felt so damn good."

His partner, Angela Mackie, a middle-aged Black woman, didn't take well to his racist comments. In fact, she was fed up. After witnessing several incidents of racial profiling while working alongside him, she decided it was time to go her separate way.

▼

Jaylen was driving his girlfriend, Channel, home after an amazing night out on the town when he suddenly received a call from an anonymous number. At first, he wasn't going to answer, but the number kept calling back to back. He finally picked up and what the person on the other end said nearly stopped his heart. Within 2.5 seconds, he hung up and called his brother.

Jah'mille was back at his estate, getting his feet massaged by his housemaid while smoking a blunt, eating ice cream, and binge-watching *Family Feud*.

"What's up, fool?" he answered.

"Bro! Do you remember where we bought our watches?" Jaylen asked.

"Which ones, bro? The Franck Muller, the Audemars, or are you talking about the sexy rose gold George McDaniel I just picked up?"

"I'm talking about the store we bought them from," Jaylen said.

"Okay, what about it?"

"Meet me there ASAP. I need you to hold it down while I handle this problem."

"Problem?!" Jah'mille snapped. "I'm on my way now!" He jumped up from the couch, spilling his ice cream all over the floor.

Jaylen knew exactly what to say to get his brother's undivided attention. He just prayed everything played out the way he envisioned it.

▼

Keshia was on the phone with Baby Chris' longtime butler, Dakembe. She had known him for years. Whenever she visited Africa, she stayed at their estate and Dakembe would always drive her around, pick her up, and drop her off at her discretion. She had forgotten she even had his number until now. Dakembe told her that Baby Chris never intended to donate more than a million dollars. He was only saying a hundred million to piss off Imani because he knew how money-hungry she was. He said Chris truly wanted her to come to Africa so she could see the new city and the beautiful estate he'd just purchased on the Madagascar River for her and their son, Christopher. He wanted to end their debacle on a good note.

But according to him, Imani burst into the estate yelling, screaming, and calling Chris all types of names as if she were trying to provoke him. He heard Chris say that Imani reminded him of another woman named Kandy. Then, came a loud smack... and a thump, like something hit the floor. That's when Dakembe got the hell out of dodge. He was outside when he heard the two gunshots. He rushed back in to find Baby Chris lying face-down on the floor, dead. Imani was slumped over, holding her stomach, and she died minutes later.

"Unbelievable," Keshia said. "Thanks for the closure. Take care of yourself, Dakembe."

"I will. But Keshia... what am I supposed to do with Mr. Christopher's cars and the estate?"

"You worked for him for 10 years, right?"

"Almost twelve," he replied.

"Then, it's yours. You earned it," she said, wishing him luck.

▼

Jah'mille stormed into the jewelry store they owned ready to catch some smoke. He marched to the back and suddenly, Jaylen appeared from around the corner. He looked Jah'mille square in the eyes and said, "You're being followed by the Feds until a warrant is secured for your arrest. Let's change clothes and switch phones. Yours is tapped. I've already scheduled your flight out to Africa. You've got exactly two hours to get to the Kennedy private airstrip in South Houston. The flight should be waiting on the tarmac." He handed Jah'mille the ticket and his car keys. "I love you, bro. I'm proud of everything you've done to become a better man. I'll see you back in the motherland."

They embraced for what felt like forever. Then, Jaylen exited the store wearing Jah'mille's clothes. He climbed into Jah'mille's vehicle and drove off. His plan was to separate the Feds and local police from his brother. He hit the interstate heading north. In the rearview mirror, he spotted two black SUVs and a state trooper tailing him.

Jah'mille waited five minutes before exiting the store. He jumped into Jaylen's Lamborghini truck and looked over at Channel, who was applying lip gloss in the passenger seat. She glanced at the jewelry and the strong smell of marijuana and instantly knew this wasn't Jaylen.

"What's going on?" she asked.

"You're gonna have to ride with me to the airport," Jah'mille said.

She didn't ask any more questions. She just leaned back and listened to the Lil Baby soundtrack blasting through the Bose speakers and watched her boyfriend's twin light up another blunt as he sped toward their destination.

Agent Vick finally got the arrest warrant sealed by the federal judge to apprehend Jah'mille Davis. So, he called the

Dallas-Fort Worth fugitive task force and gave them the green light to pursue the fugitive by any means...dead or alive. Jaylen, unaware of the severity of the warrant, kept driving the speed limit. All he cared about was getting his brother as far away as possible.

After twenty minutes and three counties, Jaylen looked in the rearview and saw a swarm of police vehicles. He had no plans on stopping. He was going to push it to the limit. He already had his excuse lined up because racial profiling had been rampant in Houston lately. He was a Black man driving a $350,000 Lamborghini Aventador and he feared for his life.

The road spikes were just ahead when Jaylen spotted them. He quickly swerved, hitting the gas, and took off, reaching 100 mph in thirty seconds, and 200 mph in sixty. Multiple units gave chase, but quickly realized his Lamborghini Aventador outpaced them all. They called for aerial support.

FBI and state troopers issued a 10-40 alert. Jaylen's vehicle was now labeled a public threat and was to be stopped by any means necessary. His high-speed pursuit aired across Dallas–Fort Worth news stations and CNN's nightly news.

Agent Mackie watched from her hotel room, silently crossing her fingers—hoping he made it out.

Keshia finally gathered the confidence to face Montano. She flew in her private Learjet over five thousand miles and drove another 200 miles through the dense forest of Mexico to reach his lavish ranch estate. Surrounded by armed security guards at every turn, she walked the long corridor until she reached the South Wing. There, she found Montano playing a game of horseshoes with ten-pound solid gold and platinum horseshoes while salsa music played in the background featuring Selena's greatest hits.

"Keshia!" he said, surprised. "How have you been?"
"Not well," she replied.
"Have a seat. Would you like something to drink?"
"Yes...something strong, please."

After taking a shot, Keshia told him everything about her best friend getting killed and leaving her to raise her son. She explained she was the closest thing he had left to family and pleaded with Montano to free her. "I had plans to pay you back, with interest," she said. "I hoped that would buy me the freedom to raise my nephew, but things didn't go as planned."

Montano sensed her honesty. He also knew she understood the rules of his cartel, but he admired her boldness. No one had ever asked him for such a favor. Still, he wasn't his father, Caesar, who ruled with an iron fist. He was *El Jefe* now and he bent and broke the rules as he pleased.

He looked her in the face and said, "You're free to go and raise your nephew. Forget the debt, but if I find out you're pushing even a nickel rock in the park, I'm coming to kill you. That's your only warning." Then he added, "Other than that, I'm looking forward to visiting your location."

As he walked her to the door, Keshia said nervously, "Thank you. I won't let you down."

Jah'mille made it safely to the airport and onto his jet. He texted Jaylen that he'd arrived. Moments later, his phone rang. It was Jaylen.

"I'm in a high-speed pursuit," Jaylen said. "I just wanted to make sure you were on the plane before I pull over."

Jah'mille laughed. "Thanks, bro. Your plan worked perfectly. I'll be high in the sky in two minutes, on my way back to the motherland."

"Yeah, and I've got a suspension and a fat NFL fine coming my way too!" Jaylen joked.

"That's light. We dumb rich, fool," Jah'mille replied.

"Love you, bro," Jaylen said, laughing. "I'll see you soon."

As soon as the call ended, Jaylen heard a loud bang.

Rick arrived in Miami dressed in all white, wearing Versace sunglasses, a ten-inch platinum Cuban link, and a Presidential Oyster Rolex. He rented a black Eddie Bauer Ford

Excursion with a chauffeur. He was smart enough to look the part. It was a mild, sunny afternoon and one of the scheduled pickup days for Imani's money.

The Boobie Boys, a Haitian gang, ran the city's drug operations. Their leader, Donjuan, a Zoe Pound OG, had come to Carroll City on a banana boat when he was ten. His parents died of dehydration on the way. He watched their bodies tossed into the ocean like shark bait. Whatever food and water they had, they gave to him so he could survive and make it to the free world. So, Donjuan never took anything lightly.

Over the last decade, he and Imani had become close, trusted business partners. Donjuan was waiting at the designated spot. Rick pulled up beside his white Cadillac truck. He got out, opened his trunk, and then entered Donjuan's vehicle.

"Wah gwaan," Donjuan said, shaking Rick's hand.

"Peace and love," Rick replied.

"How my gal been?"

"Man, she keeps me busy every day. She just went to Greece. No clue when she's coming back, but everything's everything until then."

"F'sho," Donjuan said, pointing to Rick's vehicle. Rick turned to see two men loading large duffle bags into the back. That's 20 million...all hundreds. I'll have another package ready on the next pickup day," Donjuan said.

"And just to be sure, what day do you have?" Rick asked.

"Next month on the third. Behind Johnny's Pizza on 183 and Charles. Right?"

"You better bet it."

Rick walked to the truck, unzipped one of the bags, and casually flipped through the money like it was nothing new. He looked up and saw Donjuan watching him closely.

"Until we meet again," Rick said, getting in and signaling his driver.

Back at his destination, Rick sat thinking.

He could take this 20 million dollar lick and disappear and live off-grid with his family forever, but then he thought about what he could do with 40 million.

"Just one more," he whispered, staring at the duffle bags stuffed with millions.

# FIVE

Jaylen's Lamborghini Aventador was rammed by a caged H5 Hummer police vehicle from his blind side, causing it to flip over several times before flying off the main interstate and crashing into a steep embankment filled with water. Authorities rushed down with their guns drawn, only to find him incapacitated and bleeding from the mouth. They pulled him from the vehicle and quickly realized he wasn't breathing. The steering wheel had punctured his lungs. EMT services were dispatched, and CPR was administered until they arrived.

High in the sky aboard his Learjet, Jah'mille felt a wave of relief. He was finally free. He vowed never to step foot on American soil again. He'd gotten a little too comfortable, he thought, but out of everyone, Jaylen came through in the clutch. For real. He had so many questions he wanted to ask.

Like, how did Jaylen know the feds were tapping his phone? How did he know they were following his every move? Jah'mille loved his brother and realized just how far he went for him. Jaylen had risked his career and his freedom because he believed in him, recognized his growth, and loved him unconditionally.

▼

Kandy made it back to Cape Town and was treated like royalty the moment her heels hit the pavement. A ten-car motorcade of blacked-out Mercedes-Benzes picked her up from the airport. An hour later, she arrived at Jah'me's office building. She walked past his secretary like she didn't exist and strutted down the hallway toward the President and CEO's office. She burst through the door, rude and unbothered, only to find Rob seated behind Jah'me's desk, deep in a meeting with several of his accountants.

"So what's going on here?" she asked, scanning the room.

"We're having a business meeting," Rob replied calmly.

"What business are you referring to? And where is Jah'me?"

"He's unavailable at the moment. He has me handling his business affairs until he returns."

"There's no need for you to do that. I can handle whatever he needs done," Kandy replied sharply.

"Unfortunately, I can't allow that. I have power of attorney over the business." He glanced at his attorney, signaling him to hand Kandy the legal paperwork. She snatched it out of his hand without so much as a thank you.

She stood there, her Chanel sunglasses still on, reading the entire document for at least five minutes.

"So, what the hell happened to Jah'me that has you running his company?" she asked.

Rob stood and gestured for her to follow him. Once outside the office, he explained, "Jah'me turned himself in to the feds over two months ago."

"Huh? Turned himself in?" she said, taking off her shades, clearly shocked. "I'm not buying it."

"I have no reason to lie to you. I love Jah'me just as much as you do. Honestly, it blew my mind when he decided to do it."

"So, what was the outcome?" she asked.

"A year and a day."

"Wow!" she said. "That's the sweetest deal in cartel history, but I wouldn't expect anything less from Jah'me and his all-star team of Jewish lawyers. He always said if he ever did time, he was gonna do it on his own terms. So, where is he?"

"Florence," Rob said.

"Damn. That's an underground supermax," she replied.

"I know. I've heard. Jaylen and Jah'mille went to visit him recently and said he's doing okay."

"Well, that's good to hear. Unfortunately, I'm a fugitive and can't visit him, but he knows I love him."

"No doubt," Rob said with a chuckle, trying to ease the tension.

"But the baddest bitch is back in town," she said confidently. "And I'll be getting in touch with you soon. I'm looking to build a couple of stores locally."

"That's cool," Rob replied. "You know where to find me." He walked her back to the front entrance.

"I'm proud of you, too, Rob," she said over her shoulder. "I wouldn't have respected anyone else running my husband's billion-dollar empire, except you."

Several of her armed guards stood waiting to escort her back to her motorcade. Rob stepped back into the office and wiped the sweat from his forehead. Over the years, Kandy had become a ruthless machine. If she didn't get her way, she could snap her fingers and have her goons take out everyone in the office, but she respected Jah'me's decision, and for now, she went on her merry way. She had bigger fish to fry. All she wanted now was to find out what went wrong with her billion-dollar shipment and to learn who the hell this Rick aka, "The Money Man." really was.

Jah'mille called Rob the moment he touched down in Cape Town. Rob told him he couldn't wait to see him. It had been over a year. Jaylen had been keeping him updated on Jah'mille's growth and his journey toward positivity, but Rob needed to see it with his own eyes. If it were true, Jah'mille could be a powerful force within his father's corporate empire. Rob had always known how sharp Jah'mille was. He was business savvy, intelligent, owned several businesses, and drove a Mercedes-Benz at just fifteen years old.

When Jah'mille stepped off the Learjet, everything changed. He suddenly dropped everything he was carrying. His stomach clenched like he'd been punched, and his head started pounding harder than ever before. This pain was different. This was the worst pain of his life. His security had to help him into the Maybach. He collapsed inside and screamed in agony, as if something were eating him alive from the inside. His chauffeur didn't ask questions. He floored it to Mandela Medical Center.

Meanwhile, 5,326 miles away, Jaylen Alexander Davis was pronounced dead on arrival at 4:45 pm Eastern time at Fort Worth Medical Center in Dallas, Texas. EMT paramedics said they did everything they could to save his life. His only emergency contact was Robert Williams. When Rob got the call, he hung up stunned. For the first time in a long time, he didn't know who to call next.

Courtney called to update Kandy on her pending federal case.

"First and foremost, the Feds only have one container in their possession. You said it was five, correct?"

"Yes!!!" Kandy replied, agitated.

"The federal indictment states that you were only charged with one container."

Kandy pulled the phone away from her face, her mouth wide open and shocked that someone actually had the nerve to try her.

"A heist was pulled," she snapped, "and the only person bold enough to do it at this level is Imani's baldheaded ass! That's just the type of shit she do."

"How are you so sure it was her?" Courtney asked.

"Oh, this wouldn't be the first time she's done something like this. It's just... this time she stepped her game up with real police and customs agents, but we'll see who has the last laugh. Thanks for the information."

"No problem," Courtney replied.

**A Month Later...**

After finding out they were both deceased, Kandy and her army of rebels surrounded Baby Chris's mansion in Cape Town, South Africa, while simultaneously raiding his and Imani's mansion in Chesapeake, Virginia. Imani had phone numbers and pickup dates written in her calendar book sitting right on her nightstand. One of Kandy's lieutenants noticed and screenshotted the addresses, locations, and pickup dates for her. Kandy read through them and saw that Imani had just missed a 20 million dollar pickup earlier that week, but the next one was coming soon. She also noticed several phone numbers that looked awfully familiar. One detail stood out... the 305 area code and the *183rd and Charles* address. It had her scratching her head. Those numbers and locations looked like they belonged to her worker, DonJuan, down in Dade County. If so, she was getting closer to finding out just who had been collecting her money and ultimately, she was ready to die for the truth.

    The whole city of Cape Town was on edge when news of Jaylen's death broke. Even Jah'mille's Rude Boys were amped and ready to wreak havoc on the city. After talking with Rob, Jah'mille didn't want to be bothered by anyone. He just wanted to lie in his hospital bed and cry.

    His better half was gone.

*How? Why?*

    He asked those questions in his head a million times.

    "It's always the good ones that have to die," he whispered.

    Amazingly, the doctors couldn't find anything physically wrong with him. Still, they asked if he could stay overnight for more testing. Jah'mille didn't say a word. He didn't even have the strength to refuse. He knew Jaylen wouldn't have wanted him to act a fool. Jaylen was proud of him for changing his ways, his thoughts, and his actions. He'd sacrificed his life so Jah'mille could live free. There was no way he could ever go back to being the old him.

    The new Jah'mille was going to shock everyone and in memory of Jaylen Alexander Davis, it was totally worth it.

    Jah'me heard the news from Rob and cried crocodile tears the entire day. He blamed himself for not being there to guide and protect both Jaylen and Jah'mille, but in his grief, he made a vow... he *would* find out which officer was driving the Hummer that rammed Jaylen's Lamborghini off the interstate. He didn't care if the officer was doing his job... he killed his son. So, he too, had to die.

He looked at his calendar. He had 22 days remaining until his release. He picked up the phone for the second time that year and called Rob.

"Put everything on ice until I get out. That includes Jaylen's funeral."

Kandy received the news of Jaylen's death from Rob and was told that Jah'me had called and ordered everything paused until his release. Unexpectedly, she didn't burst into tears. She had become so numb and so cold-hearted when it came to death that even the loss of her own son didn't trigger her emotionally. She was saddened, but she charged it to the game. She understood the laws of the universe. There's no victory without sacrifice. She just didn't know how Jah'me or Jah'mille were going to handle it.

She told Rob she couldn't do anything with Jaylen's body while it was in the U.S. because the feds were watching. Rob assured her he'd be on the next flight to handle funeral arrangements. That's when Kandy asked if she could join him. He was confused, but she quickly clarified that she had some personal business to take care of outside of Jaylen's funeral.

▼

Back in the United States, an autopsy was conducted, and Rob called in to officially identify the body, which shocked the entire world. The local news reported that the driver of the 2025 Lamborghini Aventador was not a wanted fugitive, but the starting quarterback for the Dallas Cowboys, Jaylen Alexander Davis. An internal investigation was launched to determine what went wrong in this tragic incident. Officer Jack Carey was placed on paid administrative leave, pending the outcome.

Agent Vick sat at his desk laughing. They'd lost one of the good ones, but he didn't care. As many bodies as Jah'mille had on his hands, they were due.

"I gotta give it to them," he said. "They tricked the hell out of the freakin' FBI, didn't they, Agent Mackie?"

She sat at her desk and ignored him.

Agent Vick looked at her with suspicion. There was no way they could've known without a whistleblower and he planned to find out who it was...*sooner rather than later*.

▼

Rick pulled up to 183rd and Charles, as usual. He jumped out of his Ford Excursion and into the white Cadillac truck, but this time DonJuan wasn't sitting there. It was none other than the notorious **Kandy**. Rick was stunned. He looked out his window and saw several armed men surrounding the vehicle.

Kandy stared him down and said coldly, "I'm just gonna ask you once... Where is my fuckin' shipment?"

▼

Jah'me exited the prison dressed in his federally issued beige khaki pants and white Lacoste button-up shirt. Rob was there to pick him up in his 2025 Maybach 650 limited edition. It wasn't a happy homecoming because of Jaylen's death, but the two brothers embraced and headed to the airport where his private Lear jet awaited his arrival. Jah'me looked different to Rob. It was almost as if he'd gone through a transformation. It seemed as if everything...every hour and every minute...counted to him.

He asked Rob 21 questions about the business, and Rob assured him that everything was running smoothly. Rob also updated him on Imani's and BC's deaths. He knew Jah'me would've wanted to give them a proper funeral, but after finding out they had already been buried in the motherland, he decided to purchase their headstones. It was the least he could do.

"Like what the hell happened this past year?" Jah'me asked Rob, looking confused. "I get locked up, and everyone goes HAM!"

Rob shrugged his shoulders and replied that he'd been busy running the family business and that his ears weren't to the streets like they normally would be.

The flight from Boulder, Colorado to Dallas, Texas was a couple of hours long, so Jah'me changed clothes and had his personal barber edge him up. Then, he had his chef prepare him a steak and potato meal. He focused on positive thoughts while watching *SportsCenter* for the rest of the flight. Rob sat in the seat beside him, knowing Jah'me was masking his pain, but either way, he was going to be there for his boy, ride or die, until the wheels fell off.

▼

Rick knew he was in a heap of shit, but most of all, he knew not to play with Kandy. He looked at her and asked if he told her where the 20 million and the rest of the containers were, would she spare his life?

She looked him in his eyes and said, "I promise you, I will spare your life, Rick. I just want what's mine. Nothing more, nothing less."

"It's only two containers left," he said. "I linked up with Keshia after Imani passed away, and I had to pay my dues."

*His dues?* Kandy bit her lip. She was hot. "So, you telling me all I have is two fucking containers left, Rick?"

He looked at her and confirmed her question.

"Where are they located, including the ones you gave Keshia?"

Rick nervously reached in his back pocket and retrieved an address book with the container numbers and locations. Then, he passed it to her. Kandy opened her door to exit. Suddenly, Rick stopped her and asked again if she was going to kill him or not.

She looked at him and said, "I told you I wasn't, but I never said they wouldn't. Kill his ass."

The AR-15s and AK-47 bullets from the rebels' guns riddled the vehicle and left Rick slumped over in the seat. Kandy walked over to confirm his death. She checked his pulse, then proceeded to hawk spit in his face and inside his mouth. Not once, but twice.

Jah'me arrived at Jaylen's townhouse, and to his surprise, Channel was present.

"I don't think we've met. I'm Jah'me, Jaylen's father."

"It's a pleasure to finally meet you, sir," she replied. "I just came here to collect his important information like his identification card, birth certificate, and Social Security card."

"It's all right here, sir," she said, passing him Jaylen's wallet.

Channel was a sight for sore eyes. *Jaylen did his thing, choosing her,* Jah'me thought.

"I'm just trying to move everything into storage. I didn't know if Jaylen was renting this house or not."

"He wasn't," Jah'me quickly replied. "No need for storage. If you like this townhouse, you can have it. Just do me a favor and leave it exactly the way it is. His trophies and pictures are like a memorial to me. You can also have the Lamborghini truck parked out front. I see you put a cover over it."

"Yes, sir, I did," she replied. "I didn't want anything to happen to it because I didn't know if he was making payments or leasing."

"He wasn't. It's paid for in full," Jah'me said. "I would love for you to enjoy these material items in memory of my son."

"Thank you, sir," she replied, not knowing if she should be excited or not.

"Jaylen's body will be buried in Africa next week, but his wake will be here in the States Saturday. Here's a check for fifty thousand dollars. It should cover your flight, food, rental, and hotel when or if you decide to come to Africa. I would like for you to have a good time on me. Africa is a beautiful country, and Cape Town, where we're from, is an amazing city."

"It's crazy because y'all don't even look African," she said.

Rob and Jah'me burst out laughing.

"We hear that a lot."

"I'm looking forward to it, and thank you for everything," she said.

Jah'me gave Channel the house and car because he knew from his son's visit to the prison that Jaylen was deeply in love with her. He wanted to show her how she would've been treated if Jaylen were still alive. If it was up to him, she was going to be good anyway.

Jah'me and Rob exited the townhouse and entered the Maybach. Channel stood in the doorway and looked shocked at the massive motorcade of luxury vehicles pulling away. She wondered just who this mystery man named Jah'me really was. She pulled out her iPhone to see if she could Google him.

▼

Keshia, in fact, did meet back up with Rick. There was no way she was going to allow him to walk off into the sunset freely with four containers full of bricks. It was right after Rick's first meeting with DonJuan when she and Rick met back up. Even though she was warned not to indulge back into the drug game, there was just no way she could overlook two containers. The game came with risks.

No risk, no reward.

Montano was all the way in New Mexico, and she was in London. She could wholesale the product and be done with it within a month. At the end of the day, it was going to be what it was going to be, she thought, as she watched her cargo get loaded into several U-Haul trucks and sent on their way to different destinations.

# **SIX**

The wake was beautiful. Hundreds of flowers and balloons filled the front of the church, which made it hard to move around. The overwhelming support from the public, his football team, and close family friends, like Uncle Rob and Uncle Meech, made the moment even more heartfelt. Jaylen's casket was 24-karat solid gold. He was dressed in a pair of Chrome Hearts jeans with the matching shirt, Lou Boutin spiked Chucks, and a custom-designed AP Richard Mille watch glittering on his left wrist. He had on a pair of flawless S1 princess-cut diamonds that sparkled in both ears. He actually looked as if he were just sleeping peacefully.

Uninvited, Agent Vick attended the wake hoping to see Kandy or Jah'mille, but they were smart. They stayed in Africa and attended via satellite. Rob told Agent Vick he wasn't welcome and to respect the family's grief. Still, on his way out, Vick stopped at the television screen to get a look at Jah'mille and Kandy's faces. As soon as they saw him, they both raised their middle fingers in sync. Vick laughed and returned the gesture.

"You niggers," he muttered under his breath just loud enough for Jah'me to hear.

Upset by the blatant disrespect, Jah'me walked over calmly.

"Sir, I need you to vacate the premises," he said.

Agent Vick sneered. "I'm not done with you. You're harboring two fugitives. That's a felony," he said, pointing at the television.

"You do know they're on a television screen, right?" Jah'me replied. "Harboring means to provide refuge." He shook his head as he escorted Vick out the door.

The wake lasted almost three hours. As people began exiting the church, Agent Vick sat in his rental black Cadillac Escalade to blend in with the line of luxury vehicles. He was snapping photos of attendees when suddenly, he froze. Coffee nearly spilled all over him as he fumbled to focus his lens.

It couldn't be.

Zooming in, he confirmed it. The whistleblower was Agent Angela Mackie.

▼

It was a beautiful Friday evening in Fort Worth, Texas. Jack Carey, the officer who rammed Jaylen's Hummer, and his family were headed to the Texas Jubilee, an annual celebration of food, fun, and family activities like pumpkin carving, face painting, and rides. The kids always looked forward to the cotton candy, Ferris wheel, teacups, and the bumper cars. Jack strapped in his daughters, Katie and Ryan, while his wife gently buckled their youngest, five-month-old Amanda, into her car seat. The kids sang Barney songs in cheerful unison.

Jack leaned over and kissed his wife. "You all ready to go have fun at the Jubilee?"

"Yes, Daddy!" the girls shouted in unison.

As soon as Jack started the car...

**BOOM!**

Thirty miles north, Agent Vick was finishing his 12-hour shift at the Dallas–Fort Worth Federal Building. He had just informed Agent Mackie of the charges he planned to file against her first thing Monday morning in Virginia. His briefcase was packed with evidence, ready for the District Attorney.

Mackie had accepted her fate. She was tired of working under a racist system anyway.

"What's the worst they can do? Fire me?" she thought.

When word came that a police officer's vehicle had exploded nearby, Agent Vick checked under his car before starting it. Tired and hungry, he thought about dinner. Divorced for three years, he lived miserably alone. When he arrived at his Airbnb, the alarm system tripped. He punched in his code, but it gave a distress signal that it was incorrect and that ADT would be calling any second now. As expected, the phone rang. He rushed to answer it.

**BOOM!**

Parked a block away, Meech saw the roof of the house blown off completely. No way he survived. He calmly drove off and called Jah'me with the good news.

Explosions went off everywhere. The 8th Precinct, where Jack Carey worked, blew up, along with the parked squad cars. The city descended into chaos. Nobody knew when, or where the next bomb would go off. Federal authorities confirmed that police were being targeted and an investigation was underway.

Meanwhile, Jah'me, Rob, Meech, and Jaylen boarded the Learjet. In minutes, they'd be airborne and headed back to Africa. Jah'me hated killing, but sometimes, it came with the territory.

▼

Keshia collected forty million dollars in just three days. She planned to pick up at least six more loads before heading back to London. After that, she promised herself–she was done.

Knowing she was walking on thin ice, she called Montano to check his temperature.
He answered casually. "I'm vacationing in Barcelona with my wife and kids. Be back in a few weeks."

She hung up, knowing she still had enough time.

After about six months, Keshia was counting money by the boatloads, and she opened several beauty salons and two Keisha's Country Cooking restaurants. She was determined to succeed, and her cocaine revenue gave her leverage. She paid top dollar and hired London's best beauticians and chefs. They were all paid up to $100 an hour. Her businesses were the talk of the town. Reservations were mandatory and had to be a week in advance. From her two legit businesses alone, she cleared an estimated hundred grand a month. Life was good and she was finally living her best life.

Back in Barcelona, Spain, Montano was sunbathing on the white sands of Cocoa Beach when he got a call from one of his inside sources about Keshia opening up several businesses throughout London. At first, he was proud to hear of her success. But when he heard the number of stores she opened in just six months, his curiosity was piqued.

He started wondering—where was the revenue coming from? Could she be laundering cartel money through her businesses? And if so, for who?

Montano ordered his source to dig deeper into Keshia's finances. He wanted a full report back immediately.

▼

**Cape Town, South Africa**

The funeral was a grand affair, held at Lincoln Financial Soccer Stadium, where over thirty thousand people came from across Africa. Kandy and Jah'mille were center stage, joined by Jah'me, Rob, Meech, and Channel, seated in the front row. Jah'mille surprised many when he stepped to the podium.

"When they asked me to speak, I didn't know where to begin. All I know is my twin brother Jaylen was loved. I'm standing here looking at this amazing crowd, filled with celebrities and Cowboys fans wearing his jersey. Thank you all for your unwavering support. My brother Jaylen will live through me. His soul, his kindness, and his loving spirit shall forever live on. He gave his life so I could live mine. His death will not be in vain." He looked down at Kandy and Jah'me. "Jaylen had a concussion back in college while playing football at Alabama."

"ROLL TIDE!" the crowd shouted.

"During that three-month coma, through God's grace, he came out. When he woke up, he told us he had dreamt that he had died visiting me on our sixteenth birthday. He said it felt real. Now he's gone...a week before our twenty-fourth birthday..." He paused and walked away from the mic.

"You got this, Jah'mille!" someone shouted.

"He took a piece of me with him. My father always said there's no growth without hurt or sacrifice. I've been renewed because of Jaylen's love and ultimate sacrifice. People still harass me for autographs. I be like, 'Don't y'all know he's dead?' They look at me like I'm the crazy one! I swear, Jaylen, I'm gonna ring your neck when I get up there, fool!"

The crowd laughed.

"To know Jaylen Alexander Davis was to love him. Your spirit will live on. Rest in paradise, big bro, until we meet again."

The crowd stood and clapped.

Kandy was at a total loss for words. She hadn't spoken since arriving. She cried in her seat. Jah'me was surprised because it had been over 20 years since he saw her shed a tear. She hid behind her Dior shades and wiped her face now and then.

Jah'me took the mic.

"First and foremost, thank you for your support during this hour of mourning. Jaylen meant so much to me... and clearly to all of you."

The crowd began chanting, "Jaylen! Jaylen!"

"Some of y'all know, some of y'all don't...we're from the Hollygrove Projects, Fourth Ward, New Orleans. Down there, we *celebrate* these homegoing's. This ain't a sad day, it's a celebration. So, let me bring out the LSU marching band to turn up. After they hit the field, we'll have another performance by one of Jaylen's favorite artists, Lil Baby!"

**One Year Later...**

Jah'me popped up unexpectedly at Channel's townhouse. He wanted to see if she had kept the house as a memorial like they agreed. To his surprise, the Lamborghini truck still had its cover on. He knocked. Channel opened the door holding a handsome baby boy. Jah'me looked at her in suspense.

She nodded. "Yes."

She explained she hadn't said anything because she wasn't sure if the baby was Jaylen's. She had broken up with her boyfriend when she and Jaylen started talking again, but she had paperwork from the DNA clinic to prove it. Jah'me read it and was overwhelmed with joy. He couldn't believe he had a grandson.

Channel handed the baby over to Jah'me. "I call him JJ. Short for Jaylen Jr.," she said.

Jah'me couldn't stop smiling. He was definitely a Davis. Jah'me could tell by his eyes, his chin bone, and that little nose.

"I see you over there examining my baby!" Channel said, laughing as she walked back in from warming up a bottle.

"So, you gave him Jaylen's entire name?" Jah'me asked.

"Of course! I wouldn't have had it any other way."

She reached into her purse and handed over the birth certificate. It read in bold letters:

**Jaylen Alexander Davis Jr.**

"Words can never explain how much I appreciate you for doing this."

A single tear flowed down Jah'me's face as he held his first-generation grandson.

"He looks just like Jaylen when he was this small. I feel like he's Jaylen reincarnated," he said.

Channel laughed. "I've honestly thought that myself, Mr. Jah'me."

"My ex-wife, Kandy, is going to go bananas when she hears that Jaylen has a baby boy. His brother Jah'mille will too. Channel, this changes the entire dynamic of our Davis family legacy."

"But how?" she asked.

"From the looks of it, baby Jaylen will become the sole heir to my empire."

▼

**One Year Later...**

Montano finally heard back. Whatever Keshia was doing, she kept it airtight. Still, the source found something interesting. They confirmed the rumors of a heist that Keshia and Imani had allegedly pulled off. According to whispers in the criminal underworld, the shipment was stolen from none other than *The Black Ghost's* ex-wife, Kandy.

"But I was led to believe that entire load was busted by customs and ATF agents," Montano said.

"We all were, but only one container out of five was seized. The other four were split between Keshia and a man named Money Man, who allegedly worked for Imani. He was killed last year. They found him in a bullet-riddled Cadillac truck. It looked like a hit. Some say Kandy ordered it. Others say it was Keshia."

"I've never heard of a chico named Money Man," Montano said bitterly. "I showed Keshia love. I let her leave my cartel with a clean slate, and this is how she repays me? By spitting in my face?"

▼

**Back in Cape Town**

Jah'mille was on site at a Davis Builders Industries construction project with his father. They were inspecting the newly renovated baseball stadium, which was the first multimillion-dollar deal Jah'mille had closed on. Dressed in an olive green and black Tom Ford double-breasted suit, fresh waves, and his father's favorite plain Jane Oyster Presidential Rolex, he carried a sleek black Tom Ford leather briefcase. Jah'mille not only looked the part of a self-made boss, he actually was one.

This deal was built by him and the company's ten board members over six months. He showed up to work daily with energy and determination. He worked eight-hour days, sometimes nonstop. He juggled calls to multiple banks, secured multimillion-dollar loans, and reinvested profits back into the business. His father had taught him well and showed him the blueprint to success, financial freedom, and generational wealth. This stadium was the manifestation of his hard work and dedication. At first glance, the stadium was breathtaking. It was a modern marvel, according to locals.

Jah'me stood beside Jah'mille, admiring the structure. "You see, son, every time you pass this stadium, you'll remember what your hard work built. That will be the fire that keeps you building and leaving your mark in this industry. Let's toast to your first multimillion-dollar deal of the new year, and to many more to come."

Jah'me's chauffeur returned with a bottle of 1942 Don Pérignon and two wine glasses. Jah'me had never been prouder. His son had taken full accountability and transformed into a leader.

"Let's also toast to growth and keeping your circle filled with people who light up when they see you. The fastest way to get where you're going is slowly. Always remember, the top of one mountain is just the bottom of another. Keep climbing."

They toasted and hugged before parting ways.

As they walked off fulfilled, Jah'me climbed into his midnight black 2025 650CL Maybach. He watched as the future CEO got into his 2025 burgundy and black Bugatti limited edition series, blasting Lil Baby's "California Breeze," Jaylen's favorite song, before speeding off.

One thing Jah'me knew for sure, Jah'mille could spend money just as fast as he made it. Then again, that was light work for a future billionaire.

▼

**Back At The Palace**

Kandy was at her $88 million secluded palace in Cape Town. It was a gift Jah'me had given her after they split. It sat atop a 100-acre mountain overlooking the city. She ran it like Fort Knox and no one got in or out without facing her army of rebels. Jah'me would visit whenever he heard Channel and Jaylen Jr. were in town.

Kandy loved being a grandmother. She did everything she could to convince Channel to move to Africa and help raise her grandchild, but when Channel refused, Kandy ordered a hit on her. It wasn't until Jah'me overheard the conversation that he stepped in and shut it down from taking place. It was cold-hearted gestures like those that made Jah'me never want to deal with her romantically ever again. Even though, at 58 years old, she could still rip the runway and stand neck and neck with the sexiest centerfolds, he knew not to open that Pandora's box again.

Just when they were changing baby Jaylen's wet pamper together, Kandy received a text. She looked at the number, then continued. A minute later, her phone rang. Jah'me could tell from her facial expression that she was aggravated by whatever she had just heard. Kandy was never good at masking her feelings because she wore them on her sleeve. She quickly exited her great room and entered the elevator to go upstairs to her master bedroom.

"Is everything okay?" Jah'me asked, catching the elevator doors before they closed.

"I'm good," she replied. "I just have to catch a quick flight out. I should be back in a day or two. Hold it down, and don't let that bitch take my grandbaby back to Texas yet."

Jah'me laughed. "Why she gotta be all that, Rachael?"

"Why you so big on protecting her, Jah'me?" she shot back.

"Because she's Jaylen's baby mother and the mother of our grandson. You can't be kidnapping her baby. She'll bring him around. Don't worry. I got this," he said.

She rolled her eyes, but in a cute way. "You coming up to my room, or are you scared of all this?"

She began unbuttoning her blouse, sticking out her tongue in a sexually provocative way.

"See, there you go being terrible," Jah'me said, looking at her in lust, wanting to take her right there. He took his hand off the elevator door, allowing it to finally shut.

Some doors, you have to be strong enough to leave shut, he thought, but with Kandy, it was always a challenge.

The Learjet landed at the London International Airport around midnight. Kandy arrived with several female assistants. They entered an all-black, bulletproof Suburban motorcade and headed toward the wealthy Cherry Hills section of London, where one of Jah'me's estates was also located. Today, they weren't visiting Jah'me. Kandy was on her way to one of Keshia's stash houses where she kept all her cash money, allegedly. Keshia had been on Kandy's radar for some time. Kandy craved the moment she would be face-to-face with her.

That moment came when Keshia decided to meet DonJuan a couple of miles from her residence. He couldn't pinpoint exactly where she lived, but he knew she was close. So for the next week, for hours on end, he watched her. On Sunday evening, around five-thirty, he spotted her blue Bentley GT driving past his vehicle and tailed her all the way back. She parked the car in her garage. That was why he couldn't pinpoint her exact location before. He decided to text Kandy. When she didn't answer, he called. He knew this was the intel she had been waiting for.

After hearing what DonJuan discovered, Kandy was on the first flight out. Once she arrived, she had her assistants break into the estate, but first, they made sure all her surveillance cameras and alarm systems were completely disabled. Upon entering, Kandy could tell it was a stash house right off the rip by looking at the decor. Everything seemed just placed. It looked more like prop furniture from a movie set. Then, she had her assistants start breaking through the drywall.

*Voilà!*

It was full of bales of cash. In fact, the entire house was filled with cash money. After about two hours of tearing down every ceiling and wall in the estate, and loading up five Suburban's with cash, it still wasn't good enough for Kandy.

Keshia entered the estate five hours later, and her mouth dropped to the floor. She had been straight-up robbed. Suddenly, she heard a set of heels walking from what sounded like her kitchen. She reached into her purse for her gun. That's when Kandy appeared and warned her that it wouldn't be a smart move. Keshia looked behind her and saw four women pointing guns in her direction.

"So, we meet again...but not under the best circumstances, huh? I guess it sucks to be you," Kandy said, laughing. "You and that dead bitch Imani have been a thorn in my ass for the past decade. Trust me, I was being nice letting both of you get to the bag. I believed in Black unity, sisterhood, and all that good shit. I grew up admiring you at one point, so I spared you when you fucked my man. Oh yeah, I know it was you. Been knew...but you still carried it like you're the Queen Bitch. There's only one and you're looking at her."

"You got your money," Keshia replied.

Feeling disrespected, Kandy smacked Keshia's earring off. Keshia knew not to swing back.

"That's not even one percent of what I would've made off just one of my containers, and you knew I knew Montano. You still pulled this stunt? He was the only one protecting you from me this entire time and you stabbed him in the back, too. This game ain't for you, Keshia. Unfortunately, your light run has come to an end."

"I have a hundred million in my offshore account, You can have it all, just don't kill me," Keshia pleaded.

"I don't come for money like you, whore!" Kandy yelled. "I'm not going to kill you, Keshia. I'm just... disappointed."

Kandy looked at her assistants.

"Y'all know what to do."

Bullets riddled Keshia's small body.

After the smoke cleared, Kandy gracefully walked over and began laughing, brutally stomping Keshia's face in with her six-inch stiletto heels. She exited the estate and called Montano.

He answered.

"It's done," she said.

"Thank you," he replied.

"The pleasure was all mine."

"So, what's next?" Montano asked.

"It was just the Westside... but now we have all of London," she said.

"Indeed," Montano replied.

# Game Recognize Game

You've just read another Uptown Classic. This story took my characters through a lot of pain in order to manifest what can happen when you're striving for greatness. For others, the price you could eventually pay for greed. Jah'mille finally realized he didn't have to be a cold-hearted killer. He could still live out his dream of becoming a successful entrepreneur while making his father proud. His devastating loss came with a valuable life lesson. He learned that there's never any growth without sacrifice, nor is there success without adversity. He would go on to dedicate the rest of his life to love, growth, and prosperity. He knew knowing his brother was proudly looking down at him.

Imani lost her life loving a drug game that could never love her back the way Baby Chris had. Unfortunately, their lack of communication and respect for one another ultimately became their downfall.

Keshia... she received a once-in-a-lifetime opportunity, yet she still fumbled the rock and allowed the lure of money and greed to get the best of her.

The scripture highlighted in her gifted Bible read: **"What does it profit a man to gain the world and lose his soul?"**

I guess she, and Imani, both can attest to that.

Lastly... Rachel Aaliyah Mendez, aka KANDY. In her demonic world, there's only room for one Queen of Cocaine and she's proven she's willing to do whatever it takes to keep it that way.

Be on the lookout for more exclusive book titles coming soon. It's been a long journey with this **Kandy Series**, but somehow, we made it happen. I promise you that I won't stop writing.

As always, shoutout to my amazing, hardworking publisher **CiCi Merie** at **Merie Visions Publications**. Without her, none of these projects would be available for your enjoyment. Thank you, CiCi, for your hard work and for allowing me to share this talent with the world.

If you're an aspiring author, be sure to look her up at **MerieVisionsPublishing@gmail.com**, and follow her on **Facebook** and **Instagram**.

And remember… **If you can put it down, it's not an Uptown Classic!**

**Uptown Classic** and **Merie Visions Publications**. We're taking over the industry **one book at a time**!!

Made in the USA
Columbia, SC
14 July 2025